LATIN BLOOD

LATIN BLOOD

The Best Crime and Detective Stories
of South America

Edited by
DONALD A. YATES

HERDER AND HERDER

1972
HERDER AND HERDER NEW YORK
232 Madison Avenue, New York 10016

ISBN: 665-00021-9
Library of Congress Catalog Card Number: 76-181010
© 1972 by Herder and Herder, Inc.
Manufactured in the United States

CONTENTS

Acknowledgments   ix

Introduction   xi

The Case of the Travelling Corpse, by *Alberto Edwards*   3

The Garden of Forking Paths, by *Jorge Luis Borges*   15

Juliet and the Magician, by *Manuel Peyrou*   29

Gambler's Tale, by *Rodolfo J. Walsh*   43

Early Morning Murder, by *V. Ayala Gauna*   51

The Twelve Figures of the World, by *H. Bustos Domecq*   63

Piropos at Midnight, by *Antonio Helú*   81

The Puzzle of the Broken Watch,
  by *María Elvira Bermúdez*   93

Far South, by *Dalmiro A. Sáenz*   111

A Scrap of Tinfoil, by *Alfonso Ferrari Amores*   121

The Case of the "Southern Arrow," by *L. A. Isla*   129

Just Lather, That's All, by *Hernando Téllez*   141

CONTENTS

The General Makes a Lovely Corpse,
by *Enrique Anderson Imbert* 149

The Dead Man Was a Lively One,
by *Pepe Martínez de la Vega* 173

Shadow of a Bird, by *Rodolfo J. Walsh* 183

Checkmate in Two Moves, by *W. I. Eisen* 201

Death and the Compass, by *Jorge Luis Borges* 211

Acknowledgments

To Editorial Pacífico for "The Case of the Travelling Corpse," by Alberto Edwards; to Enriqueta Ayala Gauna for "Early Morning Murder," by Velmiro Ayala Gauna; to Editorial Zig-Zag for "The Case of the 'Southern Arrow,'" by L. A. Isla; to Ediciones Andrea for "The Dead Man Was a Lively One," by Pepe Martínez de la Vega.

Acknowledgment is also made for permission to reprint those translations into English here included which have previously appeared in magazines and books, as follows:

Translated by Donald A. Yates: "The Garden of Forking Paths" and "Death and the Compass," from Jorge Luis Borges, *Labyrinths;* copyright 1962 by New Directions Publishing Corporation. "Juliet and the Magician," *The Saint Detective Magazine,* August 1958. "Gambler's Tale," *The Saint Detective Magazine,* February 1955. "The Twelve Figures of the World," *Texas Quarterly,* Vol. III, No. 3, Winter, 1960. "Piropos at Midnight," *The Saint Mystery Magazine,* December 1959. "The Puzzle of the Broken Watch," *The Saint Mystery Magazine,* February 1960. "A Scrap of Tinfoil," *Michigan Alumnus Quarterly Review,* Winter, 1960. "Just Lather, That's All," from *Great Spanish Tales,* copyright 1962 by Dell Publishing Co. "Shadow of a Bird," *The Saint Detective Magazine,* April 1957. "Checkmate in Two Moves," *The Saint Detective Magazine,* August 1956.

Translated by Isabel Reade: "The General Makes a Lovely Corpse," from Enrique Anderson Imbert, *The Far Side of the Mirror;* copyright 1966 by Southern Illinois University Press.

Translated by Michael G. Gafner: "Far South," *Texas Quarterly,* Winter, 1966.

INTRODUCTION

Built-in plot interest and coherence in the action!
What more did Aristotle require? The detective
story is the classical literary genre of our time.
ALFONSO REYES

I

THE above-cited partisan judgment was issued by the late Mexican writer and humanist, Alfonso Reyes, one of the most cultured and intelligent critical writers to appear in Spanish America in this century. He is but one of numerous Spanish American literary critics who have insisted on seeing in the detective story something more than an inconsequential second- or third-rate type of hack writing churned out for popular consumption. Although they are not many in number, there have been certain Spanish American authors who, in some past stage of their careers, gave more than passing attention to the writing of detective novels and short stories. Moreover, while Spanish American critics have praised the detective story and authors have cultivated it in Spanish, large reading audiences in and around the principal metropolitan centers of Spanish America have made it one of the most consistently popular types of fiction read in that part of the world. A bit of historical background can account for how this all happened.

II

There is no doubt that the great majority of detective fiction published and read in Spanish America is translated from English-language originals and therefore constitutes a type of *imported* literature. But it has attracted such a wide and constant following that it was only a matter of time before native authors of detective fiction appeared on the scene. As far back as the 1910's, for example, the success of the Sherlock Holmes stories inspired Chilean author Alberto Edwards to write a series of detective short stories about his own character, Román Calvo, whom Edwards clearly labelled as "the Chilean Sherlock Holmes."

It must be pointed out here that detective literature is essentially a luxury, a type of prose fiction aimed at entertaining a relatively sophisticated reader. Traditionally, it avoids direct contact with reality and therefore holds but little interest for peoples whose main daily concern consists of struggling with their environment to achieve a reasonable level of subsistence. Thus it is that in Spanish America, as elsewhere, the detective story prospers mainly in metropolitan areas. Moreover, in large cities there exist police forces and judicial systems to which readers can relate the stylized features of the detective story. For this reason, three predominant centers have emerged in Spanish America where virtually all native detective fiction is written and published and where most of it is read. These centers are Mexico City; Santiago, Chile; and Buenos Aires, Argentina.

There are, of course, writers from other countries who have produced detective stories, but these are isolated cases. We know, for example, of the detective tales of Lino Novás Calvo (distinguished author and perhaps the best translator of Faulkner), which appeared many years ago in the pages of the Cuban magazine *Bohemia,* published in Havana. Peru has also at least one detective fiction author: the anomymous creator of sleuth Gabriel Sotana, who first appeared in a story entitled "The Malambo Murder Case." Uruguay has produced two detective novelists in Enrique Amorim, author of *The Sleepless Murderer* (1945); and Sidney Morgan (pseudonym of Carlos A. Warren), who has published *A Body in the Chimney* (1945) and *Death in the Pentagram* (1946). However, it appears that neither of these Uruguayan authors has written detective short stories.

Rather it is in Argentina, Mexico, and Chile that most Spanish American detective stories have been written and it is in these countries that nearly all of the present seventeen selections originally appeared.

III

The use of pseudonyms and the situating of stories and novels in exotic foreign settings are quite common characteristics of detective fiction written in Spanish America. The reasons are obvious. Commercial considerations dictated that the stories written by Spanish American authors resemble as much as possible the standard Anglo-American "product" to which readers had become accustomed. Argentine author Abel Mateo has explained his acceptance of this condition, saying: "For me, one of the requirements of the detective story is an Anglo-Saxon background . . . The reading public understands that an Argentine setting is not appropriate. England and America offer the proper backgrounds for detective fiction, just as the picaresque novel has to be laid in Spain and the 'cloak-and-dagger' story set in France."

Another Argentine author, Lisardo Alonso, adds a personal anecdote. "It seems inconceivable to the Argentine public that a detective could operate on Florida Street or on the North Diagonal in Buenos Aires. For that reason, those of us who first dared to introduce the innovation of situating our stories in local settings had to cope with these prejudices, as firmly entrenched in the publisher's mind as in that of the public. The Hachette publishing firm to which I first offered *The Return of Oscar Wilde* turned it down, noting, however, that they would accept it with an English setting and a pseudonym. I agreed to change the setting but insisted on publishing the novel under my own name. One day I asked a bookseller about the novel's sales (without revealing my identity) and he replied, 'It's not selling so well as it ought to because the author is Argentine.' "

Alonso's excellent novel was published in 1947. Six years later, in the introduction to his anthology entitled *Ten Argentine Detective Stories,* Rodolfo J. Walsh was claiming that local writers had overcome the Anglo-American prejudice and that the Argentine detective story had come of age. He wrote: "The reading public has generally changed; it is now conceivable that Buenos Aires could figure as the setting for a detective story . . . It is no longer a city hostile to the novel, as was Nashville, where, according to Frank Norris, nothing of note could happen . . . until O. Henry turned it into the scene of his finest short story."

We should note here that the struggle with the prejudice over authors' names and settings disturbed only the "commercial" writers—those who wrote under contract for specific detective-novel series. First-rate Argentine authors (Borges, Bioy Casares, Peyrou, Castellani, and Anderson Imbert) chose whatever scene they wished and wrote, out of predilection and fondness for the genre, very good detective stories to which they happily signed their own names.

By 1955, Maria Elvira Bermúdez was able to claim the same achievement for the detective story in Mexico. In her anthology, *The Best Mexican Detective Stories,* all of the selections included were by Mexican authors and all had explicitly Mexican settings.

IV

The first American critic of Spanish American detective literature was the late Anthony Boucher. In 1947 he wrote for *Publishers' Weekly* an article entitled "It's Murder, Amigos" in which he astutely analyzed and evaluated the principal works of Spanish American detective fiction up to that date. His judgments still remain sound a quarter of a century later; and he missed very little in his survey.

Boucher actively undertook the publicizing of the Spanish American detective story in the United States. In the mid-forties *Ellery Queen's Mystery Magazine* published his translations of stories by the Mexican Antonio Helú, and later Boucher contributed the first (the *first*) English-language translation ever of a story by Jorge Luis Borges for the August 1948 International Issue of the Queen magazine.

It was also Boucher who alerted Queen to the excellence of Jorge Luis Borges' and Adolfo Bioy Casares' *Six Problems for don Isidro Parodi* (1946) and Antonio Helú's *The Obligation to Kill* (1946), which Queen subsequently included in his 1951 *Queen's Quorum* listing of the most important volumes of detective short stories published since 1845.

The present anthology, therefore, is in a sense the continuation of one of Tony Boucher's countless valuable projects. He and I came to this specialized field at different times and from different angles, but eventually we made contact and carried on a long and enjoyable correspondence. I have derived a lot of satisfaction from the work put into this collection, from the reading, the selection, and the translation, imagining that one of the international detective story's most talented and loyal friends, Tony Boucher, would have liked to see it.

DONALD A. YATES

LATIN BLOOD

THE CASE OF THE
TRAVELLING CORPSE
Alberto Edwards

*Alberto Edwards' Román Calvo is a virtually unknown follower
in the footsteps of Conan Doyle's Sherlock Holmes. Dozens of
English and American writers created Holmes-like detectives
during the last decade of the past century and the first twenty
years of the present one; but it is not widely known that Latin
America also produced a native Holmes-Watson partnership.
The Román Calvo stories appeared in* Pacific Magazine, *published in Santiago, Chile, between 1912 and 1920. They were
signed "Miguel Fuenzalida"—the name of the Watson-style
narrator and also the pseudonym of Edwards, who thus concealed from the public the fact that the Román Calvo stories
were authored by a former Chilean Minister of the Treasury,
Minister of Education, and Minister of Foreign Affairs. In his
later years, Edwards deserted politics and devoted himself to
journalism and the study of Chilean history. It was during this
period that he created his typically eccentric detective: Calvo
was a bit of a dandy, dressed in an extravagant manner, collected
butterflies, conducted laboratory experiments, was an authority
on genealogy and heraldry, and firmly believed that the Santiago
police were very, very backward.*

The Case of the Travelling Corpse
A L B E R T O   E D W A R D S

WHEN I read in the paper that morning the shocking details surrounding the grim discovery made at the Hotel Bologna, I knew it would only be a matter of time before some representative of the police called on me to request that I use my influence to involve Román Calvo in the investigation. My friend's reputation is constantly placing me in such circumstances. This has begun to be a bit annoying.

Well, it was just as I had assumed. Shortly before nine o'clock I was informed that Federico Ríos, one of Santiago's most capable homicide investigators, wished to speak with me.

"You don't have to tell me why you've come," I said. "Be patient!"

"I'm terribly sorry to trouble you, *señor* Fuenzalida," murmured Ríos, "but crimes such as that committed at the Hotel Bologna urgently require the assistance of your friend Calvo, and you are the only person who can manage to secure it."

"My influence, I fear, will wear thin," I replied. "It is becoming increasingly difficult to get Calvo involved in this kind of affair. He has stated repeatedly that from now on he is interested only in historical investigations, of a sort that have so far resisted all analysis. At this moment he is devoting his time to determining the true cause of one of the governmental crises that have taken place since the Balmaceda administration. I judge it would be rather difficult to drag him off to the Hotel Bologna."

"Very interesting, indeed. But don't you think *señor* Calvo might find it would weigh heavy on his conscience if his refusal were to allow to go unpunished a crime whose very design shows it to be something quite out of the ordinary—a crime,

5

moreover, doubtlessly committed by well-placed individuals, to judge from certain details and precautions? We are dealing with a very serious matter, *señor* Fuenzalida. I don't see how you can beg off . . ."

"I'm not begging off. But I do feel I must make it clear that I can in no way assure favorable results."

Moments later we were headed in a *remise* to Román Calvo's home.

The man was already up and around, but the manner in which he received us confirmed my fears.

"I have read the papers," he said to us, "and I can guess the reason for your visit. But you have wasted your time. I'll not accompany you this time."

"But *señor* Calvo," objected Ríos.

"No, my friend, it's useless. I have very good reasons for not accepting . . . Besides that, the Hotel Bologna crime holds no interest for me."

"Is that possible?"

"Murders in general no longer interest me, and this one even less so."

"When one possesses the talents you have, *señor* Calvo, it is downright unreasonable not to place them on the side of justice."

"You can stop there," interrupted Román, visibly disturbed. "One day both you and Miguel will see that I am right."

And he began tapping his fingers on the top of his desk, like a man who has finished what he had to say. We got up to take our leave, when my gifted friend stopped me with a move of his hand.

"See here, Miguel," he said to me. "You have been my biographer, so to speak, my publicist. It's only fair that you pay for your sins. Why don't you give it a try? What an opportunity!"

"What am I supposed to try?"

"Try being an amateur detective. Of course, it's really not so easy as it may seem, but a chance like this is too good to turn down. You've worked with me so often now that . . ."

I couldn't help but laugh out loud.

"What will happen to me," I said, "is what happens with the

fellows who hang around billiard tables. They see so many balls sunk that they get the idea that all they have to do is pick up the cue stick and they're as good as the best billiard player. And when they try they don't even hit the cue ball."

"Nevertheless, I'd like very much for you to give this one a try. See here, we'll make a deal. Go with *señor* Ríos to the Hotel Bologna. Examine the scene of the crime just as you have seen me do. Overlook no detail. If you do as I say, I promise that the next time you come to ask for my help, I won't refuse."

When Ríos heard this, he added his own urgings to those of Román. While he apparently had little confidence in my capacities as a detective, he nonetheless saw the chance of obtaining Román's help on some future occasion.

"I'll make a fool of myself just to please the two of you," I said at last.

*   *   *

It didn't take very long, however, for me to begin to feel the importance of my role. On the way to the Hotel Bologna, Officer Ríos gave me a detailed account of what had occurred. His version differed very little from that given in the newspapers.

Two days before, on the fourth of May at six forty-five in the evening, a coach drew up under cover of darkness before the Hotel Bologna, situated on San Pablo Street, two blocks beyond the Central Market. Even though it is not a first-rate establishment, the hotel is known for its excellent Italian cuisine and for being the scene of frequent amorous rendezvous. As would be expected, the management of the hotel is widely known for its discretion, and guests are never subjected to the slightest query or challenge.

The porter, Pedro Cornejo, recalled the details with great clarity. The two persons who got out of the hired coach in front of the hotel were a man of approximately thirty-five, well-dressed, with a flowing beard and dark glasses, and a young blond woman, tall, slender, and attractive, despite the fact that her features were partially hidden behind a veil.

The newly arrived guests requested lodging and were given a room upstairs—the now famous room 27. Their baggage consisted of three suitcases and a trunk. When the porter began to remove the latter from the coach, the man stopped him, saying: "No, we won't need that one. We'll have it shipped tomorrow to Valparaiso. We'll be sailing from there in two days." He then gave the coach driver instructions and a ten-*peso* note.

At approximately eight o'clock that evening, the bearded man reappeared alone with two of the suitcases, called for a taxi, paid the hotel bill, and left, saying that he would return later. This did not strike the porter as unusual, for he was quite accustomed to such arrangements. He assumed that the gentleman had been travelling with his lady friend and that he was now taking his own bags home, having installed his companion in the hotel.

But by two o'clock of the following afternoon not a word had been heard from the blond woman, nor had the bearded man returned. When the manager, after getting no response to his knock, cautiously entered the room—the door was unlocked—his eyes beheld a ghastly spectacle.

In the middle of the room lay two human legs, severed at the thigh. Aside from an empty suitcase that lay open on the floor, this was the only trace left by the mysterious travellers.

Fernando Ríos was placed in charge of the investigation, but his efforts to cast some light on the matter were totally frustrated by the cleverness of the author or authors of the grisly crime.

"I'd like to see Román Calvo go to work on this one," Ríos said to me, "as well as Sherlock Holmes and all the geniuses of deduction. It's not that we haven't been working on the case. It's just that we haven't discovered the slightest clue that might give the investigation some direction. It was easy to locate the coach driver who had brought the two of them to the hotel . . . He was number 375. They engaged him at six-thirty that evening from a lonely spot on Columbus Street, just east of Hornillos Lane. All of the houses in the neighborhood have been searched. Not a trace! There's not a single suspect! I've never seen anything like this before."

"And what about the trunk they sent off to Valparaiso?" I asked.

"Here's the cable I received," replied Ríos. "It was dispatched to one *doña* Ignacia Elíspem . . . no doubt a fictitious name. No one has come forward to claim it, nor will they, you can be sure. The trunk by the way was filled with stones wrapped in old newspapers."

"What about the other driver? The one who took the bearded fellow when he left the Hotel Bologna?"

"That's even stranger yet. It was car number 101. The man asked to be taken to the same spot where the first driver had picked him up—Hornillos Lane and Columbus Street. He got out there with his bags and that was the last anyone saw of him. We found the suitcases a few blocks away in a ditch, but they were empty, although the insides of both were stained with blood."

"That neighborhood must be thoroughly searched," said I, adopting a very perspicacious tone.

"We've already done that, but with no success whatever. I should mention, by the way, that it is more than likely that the criminals took these measures deliberately to throw us onto a false trail."

"But what about the legs discovered at the Hotel Bologna?"

"According to the medical examiner's report, they belonged to a slender, dark-haired male, some five feet, ten inches tall. They had been amputated by someone familiar with surgical techniques and with an instrument appropriate to the operation."

"Now *there's* an interesting fact!" I exclaimed in parody of Román Calvo.

"Well, we shall see what you can do with it," replied Ríos peevishly. "Let's take a look at the hotel."

I spent nearly an hour subjecting the room which had been the scene of the macabre discovery to a meticulous examination, but I was unable to turn up the slightest vestige of a clue. However, I was able to offer a few opinions.

"No signs of struggle," I said, after some reflection. "The legs

9

must have been brought here in the suitcases. Obviously if they had been severed here, there would be stains somewhere in the room."

"Quite right," agreed Ríos. "According to the medical report, the legs were amputated at least twenty-four hours before they were discovered."

I asked to have a word with the porter.

"Did you get a good look at the man and woman?" I asked, when he had arrived.

"Yes, of course. I always take note of things."

"Did the gentleman's beard look false to you?"

"I can't say. There was nothing unusual about it."

"And the woman. Was she disguised in any way? Was she a true blond, or could she have been wearing a wig?"

The porter shrugged.

"All I can be sure of was that her eyes were very blue. I took special note of that."

Ríos regarded me with an ironic smile.

"You've read all those questions in the morning newspapers, as well as the answers," he observed.

"Very well," I said, with as much dignity as I could muster. "I have some leads to trace. You'll be hearing from me later."

And I went out. Ríos must surely have died of laughter on the spot after I left.

*   *   *

I tried to string together some deductions, but in vain. Clear ideas refused to emerge amidst my muddled thoughts. However, I was able to construct for my own purposes a hypothesis to match the known facts. The man and woman were husband and wife; the victim had been the wife's lover. The husband, whom I imagined to be a doctor owing to his demonstrated surgical ability, had surprised the lover with his wife and had slain him then and there. This Othello, however, was not content with murder alone, but gave himself up to the extravagant revenge of dismembering the body and, in the company of his terrified wife,

10

distributing the assorted pieces around diverse spots in the city. The police had found the legs at the Hotel Bologna. As for the rest of the body . . .

Here I was engulfed in a sea of speculations. What could have happened to the other parts? Could they be on their way to Europe or America aboard a steamship? I tended to accept that idea. The bearded fellow was imaginative as well as resourceful. The masterful idea of shipping off parcels to non-existent individuals was certainly part of his repertory. There was proof enough of that in the trunk filled with stones that he had sent to Valparaiso.

But why hadn't he followed the same procedure with the legs?

I constructed a series of varying suppositions that would satisfy the conditions. And at last I believed that I had hit upon the correct one. The man and woman together had conspired to murder the third person. It was her responsibility to dispose of the legs, but, struck with fear or terror, she fled, leaving the grisly evidence behind. Yet, at the same time, it was possible that the conspirators had operated in such an incompetent fashion merely to confound the police investigation.

Out of all of this, I drew only one definite conclusion. But it seemed a significant one, and armed with it I set out for Román Calvo's home.

By luck I found him in. He was busy leafing through a huge bound volume.

"I have the case nearly solved," I exclaimed triumphantly. "All we have to do is to locate in Santiago a doctor who is married to a blond, blue-eyed, and—er, rather coquettish— woman. There can't be too many persons who fit that description, so we ought to be able to proceed rapidly by process of elimination." Sherlock Holmes had never made a declaration with more self-assurance than that which I felt at that moment.

Román Calvo smiled.

"And what if she is merely his sweetheart?"

My house of cards came tumbling down.

"Doctors, just the same as other mortals, have blond lady friends and brunette wives."

11

"But what would *you* do, then?" I asked, exasperated.

"See here," he answered, "sit down with this interesting volume and see if you can distract yourself for a while. Playing amateur detective has quite evidently upset you. Just be patient. You'll learn what I would do. Or rather what I've already done. You see, it was necessary that the official police not get wind of things and commit their characteristic blunders."

He was alluding to Ríos and his colleagues.

At that moment—precisely four o'clock—the bell rang.

"There he is now," said Román Calvo, unsuccessfully suppressing his excitement.

A good-looking young man of medium build, clean-shaven, blond and blue-eyed, was ushered into the study.

"Here he is in person," exclaimed Román. "Let me introduce you to the wife of the bearded doctor you're looking for."

"Please, sir, I beg of you. I meant no harm by it. It was just an innocent prank. Don't tell the police," said the young man imploringly.

Román Calvo burst out laughing. His attitude struck me as highly incongruous in the presence of the author of such a monstrous crime.

"Let us wait and see whether or not you're to be pardoned," said Román with complete composure. "First, I should like you to clear up a doubt entertained by this gentleman, my friend *don* Miguel de Fuenzalida, concerning the grim and unsolved crime committed at the Hotol Bologna. Just where is the rest of the body?"

"At the medical school," replied the young fellow petulantly.

"Just as I had imagined . . . Come now. Let us have the whole story."

"My friend, X—please allow me to keep his name a secret— and I are devoted readers of the *Pacific Magazine* . . . We are completely fascinated by the feats of *señor* Calvo. We—we simply wanted to see just how far his talents extended. And, well, here I am."

"Please go on," said Román. "This is most amusing."

"Since we are medical students, we were able without much

trouble to slip out of the school the two legs that were later discovered at the Hotel Bologna. There was no one else involved. I swear to it, sir. Do not ask any more questions. There is no more to the matter."

"Why it's all as clear as day," said Román. "Your friend X hid behind a set of black whiskers and you got decked out as a female in—I suspect—your sister's clothing. She is shorter than you, but with the new style, her last year's fashions suited you quite well. Please, do go on. You see how easy I'm making it for you. The foolish porter at the Hotel Bologna didn't even notice the size of your feet. That's how you can tell a man who is masquerading as a woman. On with the story!"

"But you know the whole story!"

"As a matter of fact, we do know the rest of what happened. In your interesting disguises you and your friend carried out your tasteless joke. You have already confessed the motive: to have some private entertainment at my expense. If I were a vengeful person, I'd turn you over in an instant to the authorities. There's a good reason for Article 322 being written into the Penal Code. However, this entire farce has put me into a good mood. Go on, you may leave!"

The young student didn't wait for the invitation to be repeated. Afterwards, I couldn't help but stare at Román Calvo in amazement.

"How did you find all this out?" I asked. "It's extraordinary!"

"Bah! Child's play. To fall into a deception like that, you either have to be a police officer or an inmate of a mental hospital."

"Thank you for the compliment . . ."

"There's no need for you to be so alert. But the police. How could they have thought that real culprits would behave in such a ridiculous fashion? Why indeed would anyone send a trunk full of rocks to Valparaiso while leaving in full view of all the world at the Hotel Bologna irrefutable evidence of a bloody crime? And what about the rest of the cadaver? What was supposed to have happened to it? Who was the dead man? Why was it that no one had reported a missing person?

13

"It was all much too strange and, naturally, it immediately suggested to me some medical student's prank. Only they would have been able to lay hands on those sad remains that had been severed with such scientific precision. It was a crude and callous joke, but there is nothing that can make one lose his respect for death more quickly than the practical study of anatomy.

"Those two boys wanted to make a fool of me," he continued. "The idea is not exactly original, and other detectives have fallen victim to similar schemes, especially those who have impetuous friends who publicize their exploits to the four winds."

"But how were you able to locate the guilty party?" I asked, somewhat piqued.

"Nothing could have been simpler. By her eyes."

"I don't understand."

"By the blue eyes of our presumed female. There was no doubt in my mind that we were dealing with disguised students, one using whiskers and the other women's clothing. The hapless boys overlooked the fact that those blue eyes were an extremely valuable clue. You may not know that only five and one-half percent of all Chileans have blue eyes. As a result of my inquiries at the university, it turned out that among the medical students only eighteen shared that rather unusual feature. Of those eighteen, three had full beards, eight had moustaches and only seven were clean-shaven, having no facial hair. Of those seven, three are so homely-looking that it is inconceivable that any of them could have masqueraded as a woman with any degree of success. Of the remaining four, one was almost six feet tall—rather too much for the feminine sex—while another was quite fat, and the woman at the Hotel Bologna was slender. The third suspect was a rather serious, tranquil, and timid fellow. The fourth . . . was our man.

"I simply wrote him a note in which I threatened to expose him to the police unless he presented himself here today at four o'clock sharp. You have seen the result."

THE GARDEN OF FORKING PATHS
Jorge Luis Borges

There is no writer more celebrated in Spanish America today—including even its two recent Nobel Prize winners, Guatemalan novelist Miguel Angel Asturias (1967) and Chilean poet Pablo Neruda (1971)—than the Argentine poet, essayist, and short-story writer, Jorge Luis Borges. His fame is genuinely world-wide, his literary honors and awards are countless, and there can be no doubt that he has profoundly influenced the development of contemporary Spanish American prose writing. Borges has also been for half a century a faithful devotee of detective fiction. His preference has been almost exclusively for English writers, but the name of Ellery Queen appears frequently in his essays, stories, lectures, and autobiographical notes. Aside from many other accomplishments in the field (to be noted later), Borges has written two extraordinary stories that could not justifiably be excluded from this collection—one a tale of crime, the other a detective story. The first of these is "The Garden of Forking Paths," an early Borges story that provided the title for his first volume of short stories in 1941. It was also the first Borges tale ever translated and published in English, appearing in the 1948 International Issue of Ellery Queen's Mystery Magazine, *in Anthony Boucher's translation. Borges writes like no one else. In his narratives, philosophical and metaphysical ideas tend to replace characterization and psychological probing. This is but one way to try to prepare the uninitiated reader for the unusual experience of reading a story by this brilliant Argentine writer.*

The Garden of Forking Paths
J O R G E   L U I S   B O R G E S

ON page 22 of Liddell Hart's *History of World War I* you will read that an attack against the Serre-Montauban line by thirteen British divisions (supported by 1400 artillery pieces), planned for the 24th of July, 1916, had to be postponed until the morning of the 29th. The torrential rains, Captain Liddell Hart comments, caused this delay, an insignificant one, to be sure.

The following statement, dictated, reread, and signed by Dr. Yu Tsun, former professor of English at the Hochschule at Tsingtao, throws an unsuspected light over the whole affair. The first two pages of the document are missing.

". . . and I hung up the receiver. Immediately afterwards, I recognized the voice that had answered in German. It was that of Captain Richard Madden. Madden's presence in Viktor Runeburg's apartment meant the end of our anxieties and—but this seemed, *or should have seemed,* very secondary to me—also the end of our lives. It meant that Runeberg had been arrested or murdered.[1] Before the sun set on that day, I would encounter the same fate. Madden was implacable. Or rather, he was obliged to be so. An Irishman at the service of England, a man accused of laxity and perhaps of treason, how could he fail to seize and be thankful for such a miraculous opportunity: the discovery, capture, maybe even the death of two agents of the

---

1. An hypothesis both hateful and odd. The Prussian spy Hans Rabener, alias Viktor Runeberg, attacked with drawn automatic the bearer of the warrant for his arrest, Captain Richard Madden. The latter, in self-defense, inflicted the wound which brought about Runeberg's death. (Editor's note.)

17

German Reich? I went up to my room; absurdly I locked the door and threw myself on my back on the narrow iron cot. Through the window I saw the familiar roofs and the cloud-shaded six o'clock sun. It seemed incredible to me that that day without premonitions or symbols should be the one of my inexorable death. In spite of my dead father, in spite of having been a child in a symmetrical garden of Hai Feng, was I—now —going to die? Then I reflected that everything happens to a man precisely, precisely *now*. Centuries of centuries and only in the present do things happen; countless men in the air, on the face of the earth, and on the sea, and all that really is happening is happening to me . . . The almost intolerable recollection of Madden's horselike face banished these wanderings. In the midst of my hatred and terror (it means nothing to me now to speak of terror, now that I have mocked Richard Madden, now that my throat yearns for the noose), it occurred to me that that tumultuous and doubtless happy warrior did not suspect that I possessed the Secret. The name of the exact location of the new British artillery park on the River Ancre. A bird streaked across the gray sky and blindly I translated it into an airplane and that airplane into many (against the French sky) annihilating the artillery station with vertical bombs. If only my mouth, before a bullet shattered it, could cry out that secret name so that it could be heard in Germany . . . My human voice was very weak. How might I make it carry to the ear of the Chief? To the ear of that sick and hateful man who knew nothing of Runeberg and me save that we were in Staffordshire and who was waiting in vain for our report in his arid office in Berlin, endlessly examining newspapers . . . I said out loud: *I must flee*. I sat up noiselessly, in a useless perfection of silence, as if Madden were already lying in wait for me. Something—perhaps the mere vain ostentation of proving that my resources were nil—made me look through my pockets. I found what I knew I would find. The American watch, the nickel chain and the square coin, the key ring with the incriminating useless keys to Runeberg's apartment, the notebook, a letter which I resolved to destroy immediately (and which I did not destroy), a crown, two shillings and a few pence, the red-and-blue pencil, the handkerchief, the revolver with one bullet. Absurdly, I took it in my hand and weighed it in order to inspire courage within myself. Vaguely I thought that a pistol report can be heard at a great distance. In ten minutes my plan was perfected. The telephone book listed the name of the only person capable of transmitting the message; he lived in a suburb of Fenton, less than a half hour's train ride away.

"I am a cowardly man. I say it now, now that I have carried to its end a plan whose perilous nature no one can deny. I know its execution was terrible. I didn't do it for Germany, no. I care nothing for a barbarous country which imposed upon me the abjection of being a spy. Besides, I know of a man from England —a modest man—who for me is no less great than Goethe. I talked with him for scarcely an hour, but during that hour he was Goethe . . . I did it because I sensed that the Chief somehow feared people of my race—for the innumerable ancestors who merge within me. I wanted to prove to him that a yellow man could save his armies. Besides, I had to flee from Captain Madden. I dressed silently, bade farewell to myself in the mirror, went downstairs, scrutinized the peaceful street, and went out. The station was not far from my home, but I judged it wise to take a cab. I argued that in this way I ran less risk of being recognized; the fact is that in the deserted street I felt myself visible and vulnerable, infinitely so. I remember that I told the cab driver to stop a short distance before the main entrance. I got out with voluntary, almost painful slowness; I was going to the village of Ashgrove but I bought a ticket for a more distant station. The train left within a very few minutes, at eight-fifty. I hurried; the next one would leave at nine-thirty. There was hardly a soul on the platform. I went through the coaches; I remember a few farmers, a woman dressed in mourning, a young boy who was reading with fervor the *Annals* of Tacitus, a wounded and happy soldier. The coaches jerked forward at last. A man whom I recognized ran in vain to the end of the platform. It was Captain Richard Madden. Shattered, trembling, I shrank into the far corner of the seat, away from the dreaded window.

"From this broken state I passed into an almost abject felicity.

19

I told myself that the duel had already begun and that I had won the first encounter by frustrating, even if for 40 minutes, even if by a stroke of fate, the attack of my adversary. I argued that this slightest of victories foreshadowed a total victory. I argued (no less fallaciously) that my cowardly felicity proved that I was a man capable of carrying out the adventure successfully. From this weakness I took strength that did not abandon me. I foresee that man will resign himself each day to more atrocious undertakings; soon there will be no one but warriors and brigands; I give them this counsel: *The author of an atrocious undertaking ought to imagine that he has already accomplished it, ought to impose upon himself a future as irrevocable as the past.* Thus I proceeded as my eyes of a man already dead registered the elapsing of that day, which was perhaps the last, and the diffusion of the night. The train ran gently along, amid ash trees. It stopped, almost in the middle of the fields. No one announced the name of the station. 'Ashgrove?' I asked a few lads on the platform. 'Ashgrove,' they replied. I got off.

"A lamp enlightened the platform but the faces of the boys were in shadow. One questioned me, 'Are you going to Dr. Stephen Albert's house?' Without waiting for my answer, another said, 'The house is a long way from here, but you won't get lost if you take this road to the left and at every crossroad turn again to your left.' I tossed them a coin (my last), descended a few stone steps, and started down the solitary road. It went downhill, slowly. It was of elemental earth; overhead the branches were tangled; the low, full moon seemed to accompany me.

"For an instant, I thought that Richard Madden in some way had penetrated my desperate plan. Very quickly, I understood that that was impossible. The instructions to turn always to the left reminded me that such was the common procedure for discovering the central point of certain labyrinths: not for nothing am I the great grandson of that Ts'ui Pên who was governor of Yunnan and who renounced worldly power in order to write a novel that might be even more populous than the *Hung Lu Meng* and to construct a labyrinth in which all men would become lost. Thirteen years he dedicated to these heterogeneous tasks, but the hand of a stranger murdered him—and his novel was incoherent and no one found the labyrinth. Beneath English trees I meditated on that lost maze: I imagined it inviolate and perfect at the secret crest of a mountain; I imagined it infinite, no longer composed of octagonal kiosks and returning paths, but of rivers and provinces and kingdoms . . . I thought of a labyrinth of labyrinths, of one sinuous spreading labyrinth that would encompass the past and the future and in some way involve the stars. Absorbed in these illusory images, I forgot my destiny of one pursued. I felt myself to be, for an unknown period of time, an abstract perceiver of the world. The vague, living countryside, the moon, the remains of the day worked on me, as well as the slope of the road which eliminated any possibility of weariness. The evening was intimate, infinite. The road descended and forked among the now confused meadows. A high-pitched, almost syllabic music approached and receded in the shifting of the wind, dimmed by leaves and distance. I thought that a man can be an enemy of other men, of the moments of other men, but not of a country: not of fireflies, words, gardens, streams of water, sunsets. Thus I arrived before a tall, rusty gate. Between the iron bars I made out a poplar grove and a pavilion. I understood suddenly two things, the first trivial, the second almost unbelievable: the music came from the pavilion, and the music was Chinese. For precisely that reason I had openly accepted it without paying it any heed. I do not remember whether there was a bell or whether I knocked with my hand. The sparkling of the music continued.

"From the rear of the house within a lantern approached: a lantern that the trees sometimes striped and sometimes eclipsed, a paper lantern that had the form of a drum and the color of the moon. A tall man bore it. I didn't see his face for the light blinded me. He opened the door and said slowly, in my own language: 'I see that the pious Hsi P'êng persists in correcting my solitude. You no doubt wish to see the garden?'

"I recognized the name of one of our consuls and I replied, disconcerted, 'The garden?'

" 'The garden of forking paths.'

21

"Something stirred in my memory and I uttered with incomprehensible certainty, 'The garden of my ancestor Ts'ui Pên.'

" 'Your ancestor? Your illustrious ancestor? Come in.'

"The damp path zigzagged like those of my childhood. We came to a library of Eastern and Western books. I recognized bound in yellow silk several volumes of the *Lost Encyclopedia,* edited by the Third Emperor of the Luminous Dynasty but never printed. The record on the phonograph revolved next to a bronze phoenix. I also recall a *famille rose* vase and another, many centuries older, of that shade of blue which our craftsmen copied from the potters of Persia . . .

"Stephen Albert observed me with a smile. He was, as I have said, very tall, sharp-featured, with gray eyes and a gray beard. There was something of a priest about him; and also something of a sailor. He later told me that he had been a missionary in Tientsin 'before aspiring to become a Sinologist.'

"We sat down—I on a long, low divan, he with his back to the window and a tall circular clock. I calculated that my pursuer, Richard Madden, could not arrive for at least an hour. My irrevocable determination could wait.

" 'An astounding fate, that of Ts'ui Pên,' Stephen Albert said. 'Governor of his native province, learned in astronomy, in astrology, and in the tireless interpretation of the canonical books, chess player, famous poet, and calligrapher—he abandoned all this in order to compose a book and a maze. He renounced the pleasures of both tyranny and justice, of his populous couch, of his banquets, and even of erudition—all to close himself up for thirteen years in the Pavilion of Limpid Solitude. When he died, his heirs found nothing save chaotic manuscripts. His family, as you may be aware, wished to condemn them to the fire; but his executor—a Taoist or Buddhist monk—insisted on their publication.'

" 'We descendants of Ts'ui Pên,' I replied, 'continue to curse that monk. Their publication was senseless. The book is an indeterminate heap of contradictory drafts. I examined it once: in the third chapter the hero dies, in the fourth he is alive. As for the other undertaking of Ts'ui Pên, his labyrinth . . .'

22

" 'Here is Ts'ui Pên's labyrinth,' he said, indicating a tall, lacquered desk.

" 'An ivory labyrinth!' I exclaimed. 'A minimum labyrinth.'

" 'A labyrinth of symbols,' he corrected. 'An invisible labyrinth of time. To me, a barbarous Englishman, has been entrusted the revelation of this diaphanous mystery. After more than a hundred years, the details are irretrievable; but it is not hard to conjecture what happened. Ts'ui Pên must have said once: *I am withdrawing to write a book. And another time: I am withdrawing to construct a labyrinth.* Everyone imagined two works; to no one did it occur that the book and the maze were one and the same thing. The Pavilion of Limpid Solitude stood in the center of a garden that was perhaps intricate in its design; that circumstance could have suggested to the heirs a physical labyrinth. Ts'ui Pên died; no one in the vast territories that were his came upon the labyrinth; the confusion of the novel suggested to me that *it* was the maze. Two circumstances gave me the correct solution of the problem. One: the curious legend that Ts'ui Pên had planned to create a labyrinth which would be strictly infinite. The other: a fragment of a letter I discovered.'

"Albert rose. He turned his back on me for a moment; he opened a drawer of the black and gold desk. He faced me and in his hands he held a sheet of paper that had once been crimson, but was now pink and tenuous and cross-sectioned. The fame of Ts'ui Pên as a calligrapher had been justly won. I read, uncomprehendingly and with fervor, these words written with a minute brush by a man of my blood: *I leave to the various futures (not to all) my garden of forking paths.* Wordlessly, I returned the sheet. Albert continued:

" 'Before unearthing this letter, I had questioned myself about the ways in which a book can be infinite. I could think of nothing other than a cyclic volume, a circular one. A book whose last page was identical with the first, a book which had the possibility of continuing indefinitely. I remembered too that night which is at the middle of the *Thousand and One Nights* when Scheherazade (through a magical oversight of the copyist) begins to relate word for word the story of the Thousand and One Nights,

23

establishing the risk of coming once again to the night when she must repeat it, and thus on to infinity. I imagined as well a Platonic, hereditary work, transmitted from father to son, in which each new individual adds a chapter or corrects with pious care the pages of his elders. These conjectures diverted me; but none seemed to correspond, not even remotely, to the contradictory chapters of Ts'ui Pên. In the midst of this perplexity, I received from Oxford the manuscript you have examined. I lingered, naturally, on the sentence: *I leave to the various futures (not to all) my garden of forking paths.* Almost instantly, I understood: 'the garden of forking paths' was the chaotic novel; the phrase 'the various futures (not to all)' suggested to me the forking in time, not in space. A broad rereading of the work confirmed the theory. In all fictional works, each time a man is confronted with several alternatives, he chooses one and eliminates the others; in the fiction of Ts'ui Pên, he chooses—simultaneously—all of them. *He creates,* in this way, diverse futures, diverse times which themselves also proliferate and fork. Here, then, is the explanation of the novel's contradictions. Fang, let us say, has a secret; a stranger calls at his door; Fang resolves to kill him. Naturally, there are several possible outcomes: Fang can kill the intruder, the intruder can kill Fang, they both can escape, they both can die, and so forth. In the work of Ts'ui Pên, all possible outcomes occur; each one is the point of departure for other forkings. Sometimes, the paths of this labyrinth converge: for example, you arrive at this house, but in one of the possible pasts you are my enemy, in another, my friend. If you will resign yourself to my incurable pronunciation, we shall read a few pages.'

"His face, within the vivid circle of the lamplight, was unquestionably that of an old man, but with something unalterable about it, even immortal. He read with slow precision two versions of the same epic chapter. In the first, an army marches to a battle across a lonely mountain; the horror of the rocks and shadows makes the men undervalue their lives and they gain an easy victory. In the second, the same army traverses a palace where a great festival is taking place; the resplendent battle

24

seems to them a continuation of the celebration and they win the victory. I listened with proper veneration to these ancient narratives, perhaps less admirable in themselves than in the fact that they had been created by my blood and were being restored to me by a man of a remote empire, in the course of a desperate adventure, on a Western isle. I remember the last words, repeated in each version like a secret commandment: *Thus fought the heroes, tranquil their admirable hearts, violent their swords, resigned to kill and to die.*

"From that moment on, I felt about me and within my dark body an invisible, intangible swarming. Not the swarming of the divergent, parallel, and finally coalescent armies, but a more inaccessible, more intimate agitation that they in some manner prefigured. Stephen Albert continued:

" 'I don't believe that your illustrious ancestor played idly with these variations. I don't consider it credible that he would sacrifice thirteen years to the infinite execution of a rhetorical experiment. In your country, the novel is a subsidiary form of literature; in Ts'ui Pên's time it was a despicable form. Ts'ui Pên was a brilliant novelist, but he was also a man of letters who doubtless did not consider himself a mere novelist. The testimony of his contemporaries proclaims—and his life fully confirms—his metaphysical and mystical interests. Philosophic controversy usurps a good part of the novel. I know that of all problems, none disturbed him so greatly nor worked upon him so much as the abysmal problem of time. Now, the latter is the only problem that does not figure in the pages of the *Garden.* He does not even use the word that signifies *time.* How do you explain this voluntary omission?'

"I proposed several solutions—all unsatisfactory. We discussed them. Finally, Stephen Albert said to me:

" 'In a riddle whose answer is chess, what is the only prohibited word?'

"I thought a moment and replied, 'The word *chess.*'

" 'Precisely,' said Albert. '*The Garden of Forking Paths* is an enormous riddle, or parable, whose theme is time; this recondite cause prohibits its mention. To omit a word always, to resort to

25

inept metaphors and obvious periphrases, is perhaps the most emphatic way of stressing it. That is the tortuous method preferred, in each of the meanderings of his indefatigable novel, by the oblique Ts'ui Pên. I have compared hundreds of manuscripts, I have corrected the errors that the negligence of the copyists has introduced, I have guessed the plan of this chaos, I have re-established—I believe I have re-established—the primordial organization, I have translated the entire work: it is clear to me that not once does he employ the word *time*. The explanation is obvious: *The Garden of Forking Paths* is an incomplete, but not false, image of the universe as Ts'ui Pên conceived it. In contrast to Newton and Schopenhauer, your ancestor did not believe in a uniform, absolute time. He believed in an infinite series of times, in a growing, dizzying net of divergent, convergent, and parallel times. This network of times approaching one another, forking, breaking off, or unaware of one another for centuries, embraces *all* possibilities of time. We do not exist in the majority of these times; in some you exist, and not I; in others I, and not you; in others, both of us. In the present one, which a favorable fate has granted me, you have arrived at my house; in another, while crossing the garden, you found me dead; in still another, I utter these same words, but I am a mistake, a ghost.'

" 'In every one,' I pronounced, not without a tremble to my voice, 'I am grateful to you and revere you for your re-creation of the garden of Ts'ui Pên.'

" 'Not in all,' he murmured with a smile. 'Time forks perpetually towards innumerable futures. In one of them I am your enemy.'

"Once again I felt the swarming sensation of which I have spoken. It seemed to me that the humid garden that surrounded the house was infinitely saturated with invisible persons. Those persons were Albert and I, secret, busy, and multiform in other dimensions of time. I raised my eyes and the tenuous nightmare dissolved. In the yellow and black garden there was only one man; but this man was as strong as a statue . . . this man was

26

approaching along the path and he was Captain Richard Madden.

" 'The future already exists,' I replied, 'but I am your friend. Could I see the letter again?'

"Albert rose. Standing tall, he opened the drawer of the tall desk; for the moment his back was to me. I had readied the revolver. I fired with extreme caution. Albert fell uncomplainingly, immediately. I swear his death was instantaneous—a lightning stroke.

"The rest is unreal, insignificant. Madden broke in, arrested me. I have communicated to Berlin the secret name of the city they must attack. They bombed it yesterday; I read it in the same papers that offered to England the mystery of the learned Sinologist Stephen Albert who was murdered by a stranger, one Yu Tsun. The Chief had deciphered this mystery. He knew my problem was to indicate (through the uproar of the war) the city called Albert, and that I had found no other means to do so than to kill a man of that name. He does not know (no one can know) my innumerable contrition and weariness."

JULIET AND THE MAGICIAN
Manuel Peyrou

Manuel Peyrou, distinguished Argentine journalist, novelist, and short-story writer, still holds today the editorial post on the Buenos Aires newspaper, La Prensa, *that he has occupied for several decades. With one or two exceptions, no one in Latin America makes a living from creative writing and this naturally turns one's literary career into a part-time or after-hours hobby. Peyrou, a close friend of Jorge Luis Borges, began writing detective short stories—much in the style of G. K. Chesterton—in the early 1940's. His first book—*The Sleeping Sword *(1945)—was a collection of tales about Peyrou's Anglo-Argentine detective, Jorge Vane. His second book was* Thunder of the Roses *(1948), a memorable novel of suspense and detection laid in an unidentified totalitarian state. (It was written and published in Argentina during the regime of Juan Perón.) After one more collection of mixed stories of fantasy and detection,* The Night Repeated *(1953), Peyrou turned to the realistic depiction, in a series of novels, of the fabric of the Argentine life during and just after the Perón regime. The first of these,* The Rules of the Game, *is to be published in English in 1973, while* Thunder of The Roses *has recently been issued in translation by Herder and Herder.* "Juliet and the Magician," *the first Peyrou short story to appear in English, is taken from* The Night Repeated.

Juliet and the Magician
MANUEL PEYROU

THE real name of the magician Fang was not Fang, but Pedro Ignacio Gómez. He was the son of General Ignacio Gómez and nephew and grandson, respectively, of the colonel and sergeant major of the same name. His uncle, General Carballido, was one of the seven casualties of the Battle of the Arsenal, and his cousin, the son of the former, had traveled for many years through Europe to cure himself of a *surmenage* acquired during the Campaign of the Sierra. It would be easy to deduce from this that the military figures, early and contemporary, constituted the singular pride of the Gómez family; it would indeed be easy, but incorrect, because the family also numbered priests in sufficient quantity to reinforce its vanity.

The life of the boy Pedro Ignacio was divided between the awe of marching military files and the practice of religion. He helped with mass in the parish of another of his uncles, Father Gómez, widely known for his generous and liberal nature.

This precocious liturgy was of undeniable importance in young Pedro's life. He was a child; however, he believed not in symbols but rather in realities. With the passage of time he began to suspect that all these matters resembled magic, and he wanted to perform more conclusive experiments; with palpable results. It would serve only to lengthen this story (and there is no intent to do so) to recount the times he failed in his efforts to extract a hen's egg from the mouth of Father Gómez, amid the benevolent jesting of the latter; or to record the dramatic instant when he nearly suffocated through having suddenly forgotten the system—learned through a correspondence course—of escaping from an hermetically sealed trunk. It is much better

31

to come forward to the day when, converted into Fang, he made his debut in his hometown before an astonished and enthusiastic public.

Pedro Ignacio had a somewhat yellowish skin, his eyes were slightly almond-shaped, and he had a small nose; a few elementary makeup touches and he was an acceptable Chinese.

On the death of Padre Gómez, he inherited the equivalent in *pesos* of a thousand dollars, deposited in a branch of the Banco de Santa Fe; with professional inspiration he invested a large sum in kimonos, backdrops, folding screens, and bamboo contrivances. When he disembarked in London, everyone assumed he was arriving from Shanghai. He worked for several years in the music halls of England and Scotland, and in 1930, with his tricks perfected, he appeared at the Palace, in Paris.

In Paris begins the drama that interests us. In a theatre in Montmartre at that time was playing the Great Dupré, illusionist, with his assistant, *La Belle Juliette*.

La Belle Juliette went on her afternoon off to see Fang's performance, and the fate of the Great Dupré was sealed: all of his power as illusionist was of no avail in breaking the biological charm contrived by tiny glands which conspired to make the girl's fickle heart beat faster. One December day, Juliet said good-bye to her friend and embarked with Fang for South America.

The addition of a beautiful female improved the appearance and the general effect of the spectacle; but Juliet's passion was brief. When she discovered that Fang was not Chinese she suffered an attack of fury and of insane exaltation. The truth was that she gave not a hoot for his not being Chinese; she simply could not pardon him for being South American. But Fang realized that her racial discrimination was but a pretext only. The real reason was that she had overestimated the earning power of a magician. Money was Juliet's sentimental patron. She was subjected to the last and most abject of all servilities, according to Chesterton's expression: that of wealth. She found mysterious qualities in financially powerful men, for the simple reason of their being powerful; money inferred implicit intelligence and sympathy, and, at times, even dissembled the physical aspect of men.

In 1937 appears the third character of our story. Through Juliet's intrigues, Fang's assistants had abandoned him. He placed ads in the dailies, turned to specialized employment agencies, explored infinite possibilities, but he failed to encounter the docile, quick-witted man he needed. One night in a cafe on Corrientes Street, he was approached by a small man. "I need work," he said. "I am humble and loyal." That unlikely declaration nevertheless reflected the truth. What is more, the little man later proved it with his death. He was working as a dishwasher in a restaurant at Lavalle and Montevideo. He was excited by, enchanted with magic; he had spent the twenty *pesos* he amassed by pawning a camera for the admission to see Fang's array of tricks. Besides, he was slightly jaundiced and short. With a few light touches of pencil and a thin film of ochre he would look like a Chinese. His name was Venancio Peralta. Fang made a pleasant joke: "You will go on being Venancio; it will seem like a common local nickname for a little Chinaman."

Juliet was cold, superficial, and clever. She considered that her marriage to Fang was the tragedy of her life and she was taking her revenge out on him in a thoroughly precise manner. Fang, on the other hand, found in Venancio devotion, and a practical and efficient assistant.

In December of 1940 Fang was closing out a booking at the Capital. It had been two weeks since the program had been changed. Among the tricks he included was the very widely publicized one of escaping dramatically in a few seconds from a bag which had been closed and sealed by witnesses chosen at random from the audience. Fang was placed in a large blue silk bag, the mouth of which was tied up before wax seals were affixed to the loop and knot. At this point a showy circular curtain would descend around Fang, and when it raised the magician would appear completely freed, exhibiting the knot and the seals intact. The members of the audience who had assisted in the act would search the bag and verify the undisturbed state of the fastening.

That night three men, two of whom were with their wives in

the orchestra pit and another who occupied a box, came up to the stage at the invitation of Juliet, who was wearing a very low cut black gown. Fang took off his kimono and stood clothed in long pants and a blue shirt. The bag was shown to the public and the three men examined it at length; it had no false stitches or openings. Fang put his legs into it and the others helped him get the rest of his body inside. Venancio displayed a sash and then tied it around the top of the bag; one of the men poured wax over the knot and placed a seal on it. The arrangement of the persons who surrounded Fang was as follows: with their backs to the audience were the two spectators who had come up from the main floor; then came Venancio, after him the man who came from the box, and finally, Juliet. When they had finished placing the wax seal, Venancio said: "The bird has escaped." One instant later, he clutched his hand to his breast, moved a few steps along the stage and, saying: "Go ahead; let the curtain down," disappeared offstage. Juliet followed him with a look of surprise, but went ahead and dropped the circular curtain around Fang. At the end of ten seconds she raised it to reveal Fang with the blue bag in his hand, bowing to his public.

At that moment a man came rushing out from the wings and shouted something that could not be understood. The curtains closed then and disorder broke out on the stage. Fang, Juliet, and the three men from the audience, terrified, ran towards the wings and found Venancio on the floor. One of the men claimed he was a doctor and examined him. Venancio had a dagger driven into his chest. His last words were: "Don't blame anyone; I killed myself."

The news was carried to the manager; the latter appeared, very harassed, before the audience and announced that the performance was suspended and asked the crowd to leave the theatre in an orderly fashion. A stagehand ran out into the street and returned with a policeman, who wasted ten minutes writing down trifles in a notebook. Finally, a police officer arrived and put official measures into effect. These measures were almost exclusively telephone calls in which he requested orders.

One hour later Dr. Fabian Giménez, a court judge, arrived.

34

Dr. Giménez was a man of fifty years with the signs of good living and good drinking upon him, peevish and resigned to the inconveniences of his profession. They had called him away from a meal at the Círculo de Armas and he was cursing with moderation the criminal who elected such an hour for his atrocity. He was accompanied by his secretary, García Garrido.

The three men who had come up on the stage at Juliet's invitation were Dr. Angel Cóppola, physician at a municipal hospital; Manuel Gómez Terry, an unregistered accountant; and Máximo Lilienfeld, a newspaperman.

Dr. Cóppola was a heavy man, with the stiff, elegant air of one who has just stepped out of his tailor's; he had white hair, but his face seemed young; he was carefully shaved. He gave a rapid exhibition of his scientific knowledge which devastated Gómez Terry who was familiar only with folios, mediators, distributions, and deeds, in addition to soccer. During this conversation they were observed with a certain irony by Lilienfeld, who was short, slender, blond, with bleached eyebrows and dressed in a suit of ready-made clothes. At the same time Dr. Cóppola was wondering how this little, insignificant-appearing man happened to be occupying such an honored seat *avant-scène;* he was unaware that Lilienfeld was a newspaperman.

Dr. Giménez took statements from everyone, which were summed up and transcribed by young García Garrido. The show, it seemed, had proceeded in a routine manner, save in two respects: the position of Venancio and Juliet at the moment the bag was sealed and the sentence the former uttered only a few seconds before being stabbed. According to one of the members of the company, in order to facilitate the execution of the trick, Venancio always occupied the same spot, towards the right side of the stage, and Juliet habitually took up a position opposite him, towards the left. If in the last performance they had occupied their customary spots, the order would have been the following: Cóppola and Gómez Terry, their backs to the audience; then, flanking Fang, would be Juliet, Lilienfeld, and finally Venancio. However, the order was as previously indicated: first the doctor and the accountant; then to the left of

35

both, Venancio, followed by Lilienfeld and Juliet, standing around Fang.

Fang had requested permission to retire to his dressing room, claiming to have been affected by the death of his assistant and friend; it was there that Dr. Giménez went to see him, to establish amid silk-flowered kimonos, swords without cutting edges, and strolling doves and chickens an improvised office. The death of Venancio had injected disorder into the entire company; however, Juliet occupied herself solely and unaffectedly with her gown and personal appearance.

Dr. Cóppola, with scientific pomposity, spoke first, saying:

"I suggest, Judge, that you take particular note of this detail of . . ."

He was one of those persons who repeatedly say, "I suggest" without using an appropriate tone of suggestion. The judge heard him out patiently and had his remarks recorded. Cóppola said that, according to his scientific knowledge, the only manner in which a dagger could have entered Venancio's chest at the angle observed was directly in a line from the blue bag, that is, from Fang.

Dr. Giménez conceded some credit to Cóppola's suggestion, then called Fang and initiated his questioning. The latter made clear his reticence before the questions relating to his profession, which was understandable, and he began to become nervous when he noted that a theory about the crime was floating in the atmosphere of the dressing room.

"I was inside a bag, closed, and sealed with assistance from the audience," said Fang in emphatic Spanish, now completely void of Chinese flourishes.

Dr. Giménez requested the bag and a stage hand went to look for it. It was still knotted at the top with all the wax seals intact. These were broken by the judges, with the purpose of making an examination of the interior. The material was closely woven and there were no signs of its having been perforated. Dr. Cóppola intervened again.

"Ever since my childhood," he said, "I have been fascinated by magic. Even now, burdened with responsibilities, I frequently perform tricks for my nephews and the children in my neighborhood. If the judge will permit me saying so, it is completely useless to examine that bag."

The judge turned about and regarded him with surprise.

"We want to know if there are any marks inside. Why not examine it?"

"I said *that* bag," persisted the doctor with heavy irony.

"Why do you accentuate *that* bag?"

"Because there is another one."

Fang was glaring at the doctor as if he would have liked to decimate him.

"My dear judge, I myself have performed this trick many times. Today I came to the theatre to study the execution of it and correct any of my own defects. The fact of the matter is, there are two bags. When Fang is introduced in the one which the public sees, he carries folded up in his pocket another one. Once completely inside the outer bag, and before his assistant has tied up the mouth of it, Fang takes out the second identical bag from his pocket and sticks out its upper edge so that it is this second one that is tied and sealed and not the first. In order to accomplish this the collaboration of a practised assistant is required, someone who pretends to help the witnesses from the audience in carrying out their task but who actually performs, unobserved, this fundamental part of the trick. When the curtain comes down, Fang has nothing more to do than detach one bag from the other, pulling down the first which has been lightly attached to the top of the second, hop out of it, fold it up quickly, and place it in his pocket. In this way he is able to display the second bag with the seal perfectly intact."

"Then this bag is the one Fang was initially hiding in his pocket?"

"That is right. You must find the other one."

In the face of the doctor's words, Fang's expression suddenly turned to that of a person caught cheating. He reached into his pocket and took out the missing bag, holding it out to the judge. The latter examined it at length, but it was as free of marks as the others.

"It could not be this one," the doctor said, "since generally these fellows have three or four extras."

The judge ordered a search begun to carry forth to the farthest corners of the theatre. For a solid hour Fang's bags were searched, the dressing rooms gone over from top to bottom, as well as the various sets which were piled up on the stage; but the outcome was fruitless.

Besides, the certainty that Fang used only the two bags for his trick was substantiated by the theatre manager, the stagehands, and by Juliet.

At this point, the newspaperman Lilienfeld spoke for the first time.

"Why should Venancio have said: 'The bird has escaped'?"

Then he wrinkled his bleached eyebrows and looked steadily at Fang. The latter stepped forward to explain the motive.

"I didn't hear the sentence clearly," he said, "but generally Venancio said something when he was ready to receive the mouth of the bag from me and tie it up."

"Yes, but he said 'The bird has escaped' when the bag was already sealed. . . ."

The judge had remained silent, with his gaze lost somewhere on the ceiling of the dressing room. García Garrido knew that he was thinking about his meal back at the Círculo de Armas, but the rest believed that he was concentrating on the mysterious nature of the crime. Finally, he seemed to react to something:

"There is one important fact," the judge said. "Venancio Peralta cried out before dying: 'Don't blame anyone; I killed myself.' That is attested to by Cóppola, Gómez Terry, and Lilienfeld, as well as by Fang's wife. Nothing can erase this fact. I am not unaware that a man has to be very deranged to stab himself to death in the middle of a stage. It is a spectacular act; it indicates an undisputable morbidity, whose exact character must be determined by a scientific judgment. For this reason, I don't believe we should detain ourselves any longer. I am requesting that each of you, on your word of honor, agree not to leave the capital until the judicial investigation is completed. I see no need to arrest anyone at this time."

Fang appeared effusively thankful for the doctor's words; and in the melancholy, slightly metallic eyes of Juliet shone a strange light, a sort of furtive glint. All present swore to keep themselves at the judge's disposition and the latter, excusing himself, left, followed by his secretary.

The police officer effected the removal of Venancio's body, in keeping with the judge's order, and initiated the last formal steps required for the preparation of the official summary.

At three o'clock in the morning, Dr. Cóppola, Gómez Terry, and Máximo Lilienfeld found themselves out on the street. The wives of the first two had waited for their husbands in the theatre lobby and now rejoined them. Lilienfeld's stomach was empty and he suggested that they go for a drink. Dr. Cóppola observed the journalist with the air of one performing a scientific examination and hesitated for a few moments. He believed that Lilienfeld was trying to get him to pay for a meal; besides, the idea of letting himself be seen in a public place with an individual of the newspaperman's appearance was vaguely distasteful. The encounter, a few steps further on, of an alehouse removed that burden from his mind; there he could not possibly run into anyone.

Lilienfeld ordered a beer; Gómez Terry a cup of coffee, and the doctor a soda. The women had coffee. It appeared to be a contest of economy. Presently, Lilienfeld ordered another beer and a sandwich. Dr. Cóppola had an atrocious appetite, but he contained himself; he reasoned that if he ate, the newspaperman would take advantage of this move to pass the entire bill onto him.

"It'll be less of a mess if it were suicide," opened Gómez Terry, in order to have something to say.

Lilienfeld ordered another beer and another sandwich, and while he was avidly chewing to the accompaniment of his tirelessly wrinkling eyebrows, he exclaimed:

"What nonsense! The one sure thing is that it wasn't suicide!"

"But he said 'Don't blame anyone; I killed myself.' "

"That's exactly what I mean," Lilienfeld continued. "He said: 'I killed myself,' that is to say, I made a fatal mistake, I had this

39

coming, it's my own fault, or whatever other similar statement you wish. No one has sought a logical relation between the events of tonight and these words."

"Then you have a theory? Why didn't you speak up?" questioned the doctor reproachfully.

"You were talking all the time and didn't give me a chance. Besides, the judge was regarding me with pity," said Lilienfeld. He ordered another beer, to the doctor's alarm, and continued: "There are three unusual things which break the routine tonight: Venancio says: 'The bird has escaped,' and Fang lies about the moment at which he heard these words. The truth is that he didn't *understand* the sentence very well, since if he had, the tragedy would not have occurred. In the second place, the order of the persons who surrounded Fang was altered at the last moment and Juliet switches to Venancio's place. And thirdly, Venancio says: 'Don't blame anyone; I killed myself.'

"This is the solution: Fang was driven to desperation over Juliet (for reasons which we may suspect) and plotted to murder her. However, he could not commit a common crime: everyone knew of their quarrels, apparently, and he would have been immediately under suspicion. The only solution was a murder in full view of everyone, with an unbreakable alibi for himself. He needed an accomplice for the crime in the same way that he needed one for his tricks. Venancio was his ally, virtually his slave, we understand. He accepted his benefactor's idea with enthusiasm because his devotion for Fang had inspired him to imitate the latter in even his hates and sympathies. They agreed, then, that Venancio, *after* Fang had been closed in the bag, would press a dagger into the magician's hand *from the outside,* a weapon that could be easily concealed in a fold of the material. For years they had practiced the trick and Juliet always had occupied the same spot. During the time that the bag was being sealed with wax, everyone was very close to Fang and remained so until the operation was over. Fang was able, therefore, to calculate exactly the height of Juliet's heart. The girl had perceived, perhaps by intuition, that something was being planned against her; it is not unlikely that Venancio demonstrated excessive nervousness. At the moment when they were about to tie the mouth of the bag, Juliet slipped away and occupied Venancio's position; the latter could do nothing but take the girl's spot. Confused and undecided, Venancio finally managed to communicate a warning to Fang by saying 'The bird has escaped': but the magician, nervous for the first time during a stunt, heard the voice but didn't understand the meaning. Poor Venancio paid for his loyalty with his life."

Dr. Cóppola and Gómez Terry regarded Lilienfeld for the first time with respect.

"We must advise the judge," Cóppola said.

"I would prefer that you didn't; I don't like to get mixed up in tangles with the law," replied Lilienfeld. "Besides, Fang is condemned. Juliet knows that he tried to kill her and she has him in her power. The poor fellow has no way out but suicide. Perhaps he'll invent a good trick for that one."

To the astonishment of Cóppola and Gómez Terry, Lilienfeld produced a brand new hundred *peso* note and called the waiter. He had drunk ten glasses of beer.

"Excuse me, please, but I have a matter to attend to," he said, paying the bill.

"Going home to sleep?" asked the doctor.

"No; I must go and have a few beers with a friend," he replied.

GAMBLER'S TALE
Rodolfo J. Walsh

Rodolfo J. Walsh was the first historian and critic of the Argentine detective story. In 1953 he published the anthology Ten Argentine Detective Tales *and called attention to the fact that his country alone, out of all the Spanish American republics, had created a national detective literature with its own individual style and flavor. In the same year, Walsh published* Variations in Red, *a group of three novelettes about his Buenos Aires detective, Daniel Hernández. It won for him the Municipal Prize for literature. Walsh's interest in the field of detective fiction has been expressed in a number of valuable critical articles as well as in a long series of his own stories of crime and detection. He may be considered as the most thoroughly knowledgeable and accomplished cultivator of the detective genre in his country. Walsh is represented with two stories in the present collection. The first of these, "Gambler's Tale," is an ironic little gem of a story, cleverly conceived and carried off with authority and style —and an unconscious bit of local color. Walsh's gamblers are surely dwellers on the fringes of the sprawling metropolis of Buenos Aires, and count among their number a* compadrito *or two whose existence Borges has immortalized in verse and prose.*

Gambler's Tale

RODOLFO J. WALSH

RENATO FLORES, turning a little pale, passed his checkered handkerchief across his moist brow. Then, with a slow movement, he gathered up his gains. As if determined not to be hurried, he smoothed the bills out, one by one, folded them lengthwise, and wedged them between the fingers of his right hand where they resembled another wrinkled and dirty hand entwined perpendicularly with his own.

With a studied slowness he dropped the dice into the dice-box, and began to shake them, a double crease furrowing his brow. He seemed to be wrestling with a problem that was becoming more and more difficult with every breath he drew. Finally, he shrugged his shoulders.

"Whatever you say," he proposed.

I decided then to remain a spectator solely—a role temperamentally congenial to me as a student of human folly, romantic or otherwise.

No one had remembered the lateness of the hour. Jiménez, who ran the game, watched from a distance without attempting to remind Flores that a gambler could not afford to keep late hours. Very deliberately Jesus Pereyra got up and threw a wad of money onto the table.

"Luck is luck," he said with a menacing glint in his eye. But you've got to be half-asleep for this—"

I dislike violence, and the instant I sensed the ominous implications of his words, I took possession of the corner nearest the door. But Flores lowered his eyes, and feigned ignorance.

"You've got to know how to lose," said Zúñiga, with chill

45

emphasis, laying a five-*peso* note on the table. And he added with meaningful sarcasm, "After all, it's only a game."

"Seven straight winners!" commented one of the viewers admiringly.

Flores looked him up and down.

"Gibbering fool!" he muttered.

Afterwards I tried to remember the spot occupied by each person before the hubbub began. Flores was some distance from the door, against the back wall. At the left, where the street patrol came in, was Zúñiga. Across from him, separated by the width of the billiard table, stood Pereyra.

When Pereyra got up, two or three of the others also rose. I thought it was out of interest in the game, until I saw that Pereyra had his eyes fixed on Flores' hands. The others were watching the green expanse where the dice would presently fall. But Pereyra was following only the movements of Flores' fingers.

The little pile of bets had grown. There were bills of all denominations and even some coins thrown carelessly on the table by one of the outsiders. Flores seemed to be hesitating. Finally, he cast the dice with an exaggerated flourish. Pereyra wasn't even looking at them. His eyes remained riveted on Flores' hands.

"Four!" someone exclaimed.

At that moment—precisely why I don't know—I recalled all the points that Flores had made so far: the four, the eight, the ten, the nine, the eight, the six, and again the ten . . . And now he was shooting for the four again.

The cellar was hazy with rising spirals of cigarette smoke. Flores asked Jiménez to bring him some coffee, and that fiercely scowling little man went off upstairs, mumbling.

Zúñiga smiled maliciously, watching Pereyra's angered expression. Plastered against the far wall, a drunk roused himself from time to time to babble in a thick voice, "I'll lay ten against you!"

The dice rattled in the dicebox, and then, suddenly, they were out bouncing on the table. Eight pairs of eyes followed their path.

At last, someone exclaimed, "Four!"

At that moment I lowered my head to light a cigarette. Over the table hung an electric lamp with a green shade. I didn't see the hand that smashed it into a thousand pieces, throwing the cellar into smothering darkness. But I heard the gunshot, a single deafening report ringing out in the blackness.

I made myself small in my corner. *Poor Flores! He was too lucky!* I heard something come rolling over near me, and felt it touch my hand. It was a die. Groping in the darkness I quickly found its mate.

In the midst of the tumult someone remembered the neon tubes on the ceiling. But when they came on, it wasn't Flores who was dead. Flores was standing frozen with the dice-box in his hand, his eyes dark pools of horror. At his left, doubled up in his seat, was Zúñiga with a bullet in his chest.

My first thought was: *They missed Flores and shot someone else by mistake! Nothing can happen to him tonight. His luck is too incredible.*

Two of the outsiders picked up Zúñiga, and laid him out on three chairs placed in a row. Jiménez, who had just come down with the coffee, refused to let them put him on the billiard table, for fear that an ineradicable stain would spread over its felt surface. Anyway, it was too late to do anything for unlucky Zúñiga.

Stepping over by the table I noticed that the dice on its surface spelled out a seven. Lying between them was a gleaming, thirty-eight calibre revolver with a pearl handle.

As inconspicuously as possible, I slipped over to the door, and went slowly up the stairs. Out in the street a crowd of excited onlookers had gathered, and a policeman was elbowing his way through them.

That night I remembered the dice I was carrying in my pocket —I had completely forgotten them—and I began to play alone, just for diversion. I rolled dice for half an hour without hitting a seven. I soon realized that I was playing with dice which had been very unethically numbered. One of the "educated cubes" had the five, four, and three repeated on opposite sides—the other the five, six, and one.

With such dice a man's luck could hardly fail to seem miraculous. You couldn't lose on the first throw because it would have been impossible to make up a two, three, or twelve, which are the only unlucky numbers on the first roll. And you couldn't lose on the rest because it was impossible to throw a seven, which is a loser *after* the first throw.

I remembered that Flores had made seven straight points, and almost all of them with hard numbers: the four, the eight, and ten, the nine, the eight, the six, and again the ten . . . And on the last throw he had come up with the four again. Not one single "snake-eyes" had he thrown—not one "boxcars." And in the forty odd times that I had tossed the dice, I hadn't rolled a single seven—and seven is the number that most often appears in the normal course of a game.

But, nevertheless, after the tragedy the dice on the table had read seven, instead of four, which had been the last number rolled. I can still see it clearly: a six and a one.

The following day I moved to another part of town and, perhaps with subconscious intent, misplaced the dice.

Whether or not the authorities came looking for me, I don't know. For a while I heard nothing more about the tragedy. Then, one afternoon, I read in the papers that Pereyra had confessed. According to his statement, he had realized that Flores had been cheating and had killed him in blind rage. Pereyra has been losing more than he could afford, and everyone knew that the man was a bad loser. The rage had come upon him when Flores' winnings had reached three thousand *pesos,* and he had smashed the light with one blow. But in the darkness he had aimed poorly, and instead of killing Flores he had killed Zúñiga. Curiously enough, I had reached the same conclusion myself at first.

As might have been expected, they had to let Pereyra go. He told the judge that he had been made to confess under duress, and the authorities had to admit that many points remained vague. In the dark it is easy to mistake a target, but Flores had been standing directly in front of him at a distance of three feet while Zúñiga had been far to one side. One detail especially favored him: the broken fragments from the cellar light had fallen behind him. If he had been the one to smash the light the glass would have been found on the other side of the billiard table, where Flores and Zúñiga had been standing.

The incident remained without explanation. No one had seen Pereyra smash the light. Everyone's eyes had been glued to the dice. And even if the killer had been seen, nothing had been said. I, myself, who could have seen him, had lowered my head to light a cigarette which I never did light. No prints had been found on the revolver, nor could the owner be determined. Any one of the men around the table—and there had been eight or nine—could have shot Zúñiga.

Who more than anyone else had an account to settle with Zúñiga? Well, if I had wanted to incriminate someone in a dice game, I'd sit on his left. And as I lost I'd exchange the honest dice for a pair like those I had found on the floor, put them in the dice-box, and pass them to my victim.

The man would win once and be happy. He'd win twice, three times—and he'd go right on winning. No matter how hard his opening number might be, he'd always make the point before a seven came up. If Jiménez let him, he'd win all night, *because with those dice he couldn't lose!*

Of course I wouldn't wait around to see the outcome. I'd go home to bed and the next day I'd read about it in the papers. Try to chalk up ten or fifteen points in company like that! It's good to have a little luck; to have too much luck is not good; and to help your luck along is dangerous . . .

Yes, I think that it was Flores himself who killed Zúñiga. And, in a way, he did it in self-defense. Flores killed him so that Pereyra or one of the others wouldn't kill our lucky Flores first. Zúñiga—because of some old grudge, perhaps—had slipped the crooked dice into the dice-box, and had thus condemned Flores to win all night, to cheat without knowing it. He had condemned him to death, or to betray himself by giving an explanation so humiliating that nobody would believe it.

Flores was late in realizing the deadly trick that had been played on him. At first he thought it was pure luck. Afterwards he got uneasy; and when he understood Zúñiga's evil intention, when he saw that Pereyra was ready for trouble, and was keeping his eyes on his hands to see if he'd change the dice again, he realized that he could save himself in only one way. In order to get Jiménez away from behind his chair, he persuaded him to go complaining upstairs for some coffee. Then he waited for the right moment. It came when the four showed up again, as he knew it would, and when everyone was instinctively absorbed by the dice.

Then he broke the light bulb with one blow from the dice-box, took out the revolver with his checkered handkerchief and shot Zúñiga through the heart. He left the revolver on the table, recovered the "loaded dice," and threw them on the floor. There was no time for anything else.

He didn't want it to be known that he had been cheating, even if it had been without his knowledge. So he fished in Zúñiga's pockets for the legitimate dice which the latter had taken from the dice-box and which, just as the fluorescent lights began to flicker on again, he threw on the table.

And this time he did roll with the odds, coming up with the number that most often appears—a seven, big as a house!

50

EARLY MORNING MURDER
Velmiro Ayala Gauna

Velmiro Ayala Gauna was born in the northern Argentine province of Corrientes, became a journalist there, and has subsequently devoted his career as a writer to depicting the life of the tropical region of his birth. When he created his rural "comisario" (police chief), don Frutos Gómez, he was not, technically, the first Argentine writer to situate detective stories in the vast northern reaches of his country. In 1942 a Jesuit priest by the name of Leonardo Castellani published a collection of detective stories about a provincial priest-detective named Padre Metri. The book, entitled Father Metri's Nine Deaths, *introduced an intelligent, well-educated, but down-to-earth solver of mysteries whose resemblance to Chesterton's Father Brown was unmistakable. One might even say he was the Argentine "translation" of Father Brown. Ayala Gauna's don Frutos, however, is native bred—an authentic "backwoods" sleuth whose common sense, if not his formal training, is sufficient to trap unsophisticated criminals in and around the little village of Capibara-Cué. There are two volumes of don Frutos tales and numerous others uncollected. "Early Morning Murder" is taken from* Don Frutos Gómez, Police Chief *(1960).*

Early Morning Murder
VELMIRO AYALA GAUNA

A TRAVELLING salesman who had been passing through the little provincial town in the Argentine north had handed out the almanacs free to the customers of the general store. They contained, aside from abundant advertisements, all kinds of assorted information, and Corporal Leiva, who had been honored with a copy, was seated at his desk at the local police station, reading it carefully and, from time to time, making observations to Deputy Immaculate Ojeda who was serving him maté.

He thumbed through several pages and stopped on one that listed facts related to astronomy. He fell to reading these and then, after a while, maliciously called Ojeda over to plot a practical joke to be played on Judge Arzásola who would soon be arriving in the company of Police Chief *don* Frutos Gómez.

When, moments later, the two men arrived they spied the corporal standing a few steps away from his desk, his eyes half-closed, muttering:

"By my figurings . . . it's near to five feet and nine inches."

Ojeda extracted a tape measure from his pocket, made a measurement and concluded:

"Right . . . Now let's have a look-see at what it is from here to there."

And as if he were picking his coordinates out of the air, he laid out the distance between the door frame and a nail on the wall.

"And from yonder over to here it looks like four feet and one inch."

The police officer went through the pantomime once more and determined:

53

"Same thing . . . right on the button again."

Arzásola could not restrain himself.

"It's really astonishing how you can do all that figure-toting so quickly and accurately."

"Bah! 'Tain't nothin',", replied Leiva. "Gimme somethin' harder. How's about my figurin' out for you how far a piece it is from here to the sun?"

"Ah, my friend. Those are big figures you wouldn't be able to handle."

"Now wait a sec, your honor, just let me try . . ."

The corporal stepped out into the street, glanced up at the sun rising in the east and exclaimed:

"Give, take a few feet, it must be ninety-two million, nine hundred, and fifty-six thousand miles."

Arzásola took out a notebook, checked in the back pages, and murmured in amazement to *don* Frutos who had witnessed the entire scene without comment:

"Astonishing! Do you realize he hit the distance right on the mark? It is, indeed, ninety-two million, nine hundred, and fifty-six thousand miles away. This is incredible!"

Then, from behind them, came the somber voice of Ojeda, saying:

"It's just like Sakeshpear said—'There are more things in heaven and earth, my friend, than human philosophy can imagine!' "

The judge stood transfixed, his mouth gaping, as he listened to the literary citation. But *don* Frutos, turning back, went up to Ojeda and removed from the booklet that was sticking out of his back pocket.

"Now let's see. I figure we ought to be able to find hidden someplace in here the learnin' that's all of a sudden taken charge of this fellow. Here it is. 'There are more things in heaven and . . .' "

"Ah, that explains it," said Arzásola. "It did seem more than a little strange to me that Ojeda here would be gaily spouting lines from the author of *Hamlet*."

"And over here, on another page," said *don* Frutos, "is a list of the distances between the earth and the planets and the sun . . ."

"Ha, ha, ha!" laughed Leiva. "You didn't fall for it, *don* Frutos, because you're more cadgy than a one-eyed burro. But we got the judge—hook, line, and sinker."

Arzásola was about to unleash an angry attack on the corporal when a humbly dressed individual rushed into the office.

"*Don* Frutos! Just a few minutes ago . . . I was heading out into the fields to work with *don* Paulo Stopani. And I—I found him in his vegetable garden. His head was beaten in. He's dead."

Leaving Ojeda in charge of the office, the others hurried off to the scene of the crime.

*　　*　　*

"Gringo" Stopani, as he was called, had been living in Capibara-Cué for many years. When he returned from his job as a coal stoker on a river boat, he settled down there permanently. Three years before, he had surprised his neighbors by returning from Corrientes, where he had gone to spend a few months, with a widow whom he had married after a brief courtship. With them came the woman's son, who took to spending his time hanging around the general store and weekend dances and fled manual labor as if it were the devil himself. Just a year before, however, the wife had died from an infection and the stepfather obliged the son, to the latter's great displeasure, to pitch in and help with the farm work. This, and the fact that the son persisted in his free-wheeling way of life, made for strained relations between them.

Felix Palomeque—such was the name of the stepson—was waiting for the police in the doorway of his home.

"When the *peón* brought word of what had happened," he explained, "I was still in bed. I sent him right away to fetch you . . . He's over there, in the garden, behind the houses."

They found the body lying face down alongside the newly dug

55

furrows of several plots marked off for seedbeds. The rectangles of two seed packets stood out against the dark, fresh soil, still moist with the morning dew.

"I don't reckon there's any doubt about what he died from," observed the judge. "You can see his skull's crushed in and all covered with blood."

"Boy, they really let 'im have a couple of good ones," added Leiva.

"He must have been bending over planting the seeds when someone came up behind and struck him," suggested the stepson.

Don Frutos glanced about the area for a moment before refuting the statement:

"This place is pretty much out in the open, no? Where could anyone hide who wanted to creep up and surprise him?"

"True," said the judge, "there's really no place to hide here."

"Therefore," *don* Frutos continued, "*don* Paulo had to have seen his murderer approaching. And if he didn't react to that, it must have been because . . ."

"Because why?" snapped Arzásola.

"Because he didn't distrust him. It must have been someone he knew perfectly well, like Felix."

"Me!" exclaimed the stepson. "I was in bed . . ."

"Or like you," the police chief went on, addressing the *peón* who instantly went pale.

"I swear, I swear on my mother's grave that I didn't do it," he blurted out.

"Don't worry. If you're innocent, nothing's going to happen to you. Why don't you all carry the body back to the house until the coffin's ready."

Leiva, the *peón,* and the stepson together raised the dead man and carried him home, while *done* Frutos, accompanied by the judge, examined the scene of the crime and then, following a faint trail of footsteps in the soft soil, approached the barbed wire fence that, some two hundred yards away, separated the garden from the neighboring piece of property. He stopped beside a fence post, looked across the fence, and spotted a heavy stick lying among the weeds.

"Look. There's the weapon," he said to Arzásola. "You're younger than I am. Why don't you scramble over and fetch it."

The judge complied and was back in a moment with the solid chunk of wood, a length of dried tree branch that he placed in *don* Frutos' hands. At the heaviest end could be seen reddish stains and bits of skin.

"This is what he was clubbed to death with."

"The criminal no doubt pitched it into the brush as he was running away," commented the judge.

"Hmmm," replied *don* Frutos.

They went back to the house and entered through the kitchen where they found the *peón* preparing maté. When he laid eyes on the bloody club, he closed his eyes and leaned back against the fireplace.

"Wh—where did you find it?" he asked after a moment, recovering from the shock.

"On the other side of the fence. Out that way," the police chief said, motioning with his hand. "Who lives over there?"

"*Don* José Suárez, but—oh!" he exclaimed, cutting himself off in mid-sentence.

"What's the matter, fellow?"

"It's just that the other day there was a big argument because one of ol' Suárez's horses got into the vegetable garden and trampled all over the seed beds. They yelled all kinds of things at each other and we had to pull *don* Paulo away. He wanted to fight."

"And did Suárez threaten him?"

"Did he ever! You wouldn't believe the things he said."

"For example?"

"Well, I don't recollect too clearly, but it was something like: 'You'd better be watching out for more than your plants, filthy *gringo,* because if I get my hands on you, you'll end up looking like a toad that got run over by a wagon wheel.' "

"Aha," exclaimed *don* Frutos, immediately calling the corporal over.

"Go over to the house there and bring back *don* José Suárez."

"I'm on my way, chief," Leiva replied as he hurried out.

57

Indicating a sizable dark stain on the floor, *don* Frutos asked the *peón:*

"What did you spill here?"

"I didn't do it," the *peón* answered. "It was here when I came."

"My stepfather probably spilled the tea kettle or a pan of water on the floor," interjected Palomeque, who had just come into the kitchen.

"Yes, probably so," said *don* Frutos. "Let's go into the dining room and wait for *don* José. I want to question you all together."

"How about a maté while you're waiting?" asked the *peón.*

"No. Maybe later. Just go on in."

They went on into a modestly furnished room where they drew several chairs together and sat down. Leiva promptly returned with the neighbor, an old farmer who came in with a sullen look on his wrinkled face.

"What's going on, *don* Frutos? Why am I being led around as if I was some kind of criminal?"

"Are you sure that you're not?"

"Of course I'm not. So why . . ."

"Well, then, who killed *don* Paulo?"

"*Don* Paulo, the *gringo?*"

"Yes. The same man you threatened just a few days ago."

The old farmer's head drooped and his voice came out very small. "God forgive me for the things I said to him . . . but I didn't kill him. I didn't do it."

"From the stiffness in the body, I'd calculate he was killed four or five hours ago, more or less. Around six o'clock A.M. What were you doing then, *don* José?"

"I was in bed asleep."

"What about you, Felix?"

"The same. When I heard the news I was in bed."

"And what about you, my boy?" said *don* Frutos, addressing the *peón.*

He gulped and then answered:

"I was still sleeping then."

"That's fine. But for my money, one of you wasn't sleeping,

but up and around—busy putting poor old *don* Paulo to sleep with a club. Wait right here."

Don Frutos called Leiva and conversed with him in a low tone. When he finished, he returned to his seat and Leiva went off on an errand.

"If you ask me," *don* Frutos continued, after a silence, "all three of you are suspects. You, Felix, because you stand to come into the inheritance. You, *don* José, because you threatened him something terrible. And you, my boy, because you wanted revenge. Who knows what *don* Paulo may have done to mistreat you and make you . . ."

He left the sentence unfinished, then went on.

"You first, Felix. Tell us what you know."

"There's not much to tell. Last night my stepfather told me he was going to get up early today because he wanted to plant Swiss chard and radishes."

"What vegetables did you say?"

"Swiss chard and radishes. He read in that book there, that almanac, that this was the right season. I said I'd help him but he refused. I insisted because . . ."

"Because why?"

"Because I was afraid that something might happen to him because the other day he had a terrible fight with *don* José. And you see now . . ."

"You don't really think *I* did it, do you?"

"I'm not blaming you, no. But who else could it have been?"

The old man jumped up furiously and grabbed for Felix. But Arzásola reached out and restrained him. At this point, Leiva came in and nodded at *don* Frutos.

"Before I go on, my friend, I want you to think hard. Was it actually Swiss chard and radishes that *don* Paulo told you he was going to plant?"

"Yep. There's the book that tells about it. This is the right month."

"That's right. But you, being a city boy, forgot the moon. That's why—"

"The moon?"

"Right. Your stepfather, who used to work on a boat, learned to till the soil here with us. You, on the other hand, have spent your life going to school, where you never had to do any kind of work until your father died and *don* Paulo began to make you put in a little labor in return for your daily bread."

"What's all this got to do with anything?"

"It tells me you're a liar, because the dead man would never have planted Swiss chard and radishes at the same time."

"But this *is* the right month!"

"Naturally. But one's planted at the beginning of the month and one in the middle. Plants that grow *up,* like Swiss chard, are put in with the waxing moon and those that grow *down,* like radishes, with the waning moon, while those that are grown for their seeds are planted with the full moon. Isn't that right, *don* José?"

"Absolutely, *don* Frutos!"

"Well, maybe I heard him wrong—"

"No. Because those were the kinds of seed packets we found in the seedbed."

"I can't help that. Somewhere you've made a mistake."

"Could be. But tell me now, where are your canvas sandals?"

"They were worn out and I threw them away."

"Where?"

"I—forget. Out there someplace."

"Let's have them, Leiva. Where were they?"

"Under a couple of bricks, near the outdoor oven."

Don Frutos pointed out the damp, earth-covered soles.

"If you were sleeping when your stepfather was killed, how is it that your sandals have fresh soil from the garden on them?"

Palomeque, confused, could not speak. *Don* Frutos went on.

"Listen to me. I'll tell you how it happened. This morning *don* Paulo dragged you out of bed to help him. You had an argument in the kitchen and, when the old fellow wasn't looking, you grabbed a hunk of firewood and bashed in his skull. Then you got scared and, to throw me off the track, you carried the body to the garden and tossed the club over into *don* José's property so as to throw the guilt on him. You washed the floor

60

of the kitchen to clean up the bloodstains, buried your dirty sandals, and looked in the almanac to see what could be sown. Then you picked out the seed packets and threw them beside the dead man. With all this done, you climbed back into bed and waited for the *peón* to find the body and prove you were asleep all the time."

"How did you figure all this out?" asked Suárez.

"Mainly the business of the wrong seeds and the fact that there wasn't blood around the body. Later, when I saw the floor had been washed in the kitchen, I figured that he had been killed there, and then carried out to the garden to throw off suspicion. And if this was all true, who else could it have been?"

THE TWELVE FIGURES
OF THE WORLD
H. Bustos Domecq

H. Bustos Domecq is the pseudonym of Jorge Luis Borges and Adolfo Bioy Casares, whose friendship goes back some forty years and whose literary collaboration (one of the few in Hispanic letters) dates from the moment in 1941 when they sat down to write a detective story. The result was "The Twelve Figures of the World" and the creation of a third person, another author. For the Bustos Domecq stories reflect neither Borges's style nor that of Bioy Casares. Clearly, the stories that make up Six Problems for Don Isidro Parodi *(1942), as well as all the other writings that Borges and Bioy sign with the Bustos Domecq name, are the work of a third party. Bioy's fondness for detective fiction is as great as Borges'. Together they have edited two anthologies of detective short stories and have supervised the publication in translation of a long series of detective novels for their Buenos Aires publisher, Emecé. In addition to the Isidro Parodi stories, they have written a whimsical detective novelette entitled* A Model for Death *(1945). Playfulness, humor, and satire are qualities of all the Borges-Bioy writings, as can be observed in "The Twelve Figures of the World," in which the foppish Aquiles Molinari gets his comeuppance and* don *Isidro (the only detective we know who works out of a prison cell) solves a delightfully clever murder case.*

The Twelve Figures of the World
H. BUSTOS DOMECQ
(JORGE LUIS BORGES and
ADOLFO BIOY CASARES)

I

CAPRICORN, Aquarius, Pisces, Aries, Leo, thought Aquiles Molinari as he lay sleeping. Then he experienced a moment of doubt. He saw Libra and Scorpio. He understood that he had made a mistake; he wakened, trembling.

The sun had warmed his face. On the night table, resting on the Bristol Almanac and several numbers of *La Fija,* the Tic Tac alarm clock indicated 9:40. Still repeating the signs, Molinari got up. He looked out the window. On the street corner was the stranger.

He smiled astutely. He went to the rear of his flat and returned with his razor, the shaving brush, the remains of the yellow soap, and a cup of hot water. He opened the window wide, regarded the stranger below with emphatic serenity, and slowly shaved, whistling the tango "Naipe Marcado."

Ten minutes later he was in the street, dressed in the brown suit on which he still owed the last two payments to the Grandes Sastrerías Rabuffi. He went to the corner; the stranger brusquely became interested in a lottery-drawing announcement. Molinari, well accustomed to these tiresome dissimulations, headed towards the corner of Humberto I. The bus arrived promptly, and Molinari got on. In order to simplify his pursuer's task he occupied one of the front seats. After two or three blocks he turned his head. The stranger, easily recognizable for his dark glasses, was reading a newspaper. Even before it reached downtown, the bus was full. Molinari could have gotten off without the stranger's knowledge, but he had a better scheme. He stayed on until the Palermo Brewery. Then, without looking around, he walked back in a northerly direction alongside the high wall of the Penitenciaría and entered the gardens. He considered that he was proceeding calmly, but before reaching the prison guard's post he threw down a cigarette that he had lit only moments before. He exchanged trivial words with a shirt-sleeved employee, and a jailkeeper accompanied him to Cell 273.

Four years earlier, the butcher Agustín R. Bonorino, who had attended the races at Belgrano disguised as an Italian immigrant, received a mortal head wound from a bottle. It was widely known that the Bilz bottle which struck him down had been wielded by a chap from the Pata Santa district. But since Pata Santa was a highly prized electoral factor, the police had determined that the guilty party was Isidro Parodi, whom some persons declared was a nihilist, meaning to say that he was a spiritist. In truth, Isidro Parodi was neither of the two: he was the proprietor of a barbershop on the southside and had committed the indiscretion of letting out a room to a clerk at the Eighteenth Precinct who was more than a year behind in his rent. This combination of adverse circumstances sealed Parodi's fate. The statements of the witnesses (who were from Pata Santa) were in total agreement. The judge sentenced him to twenty years in prison.

Sedentary life had affected the murderer of 1919: today he was a fortyish man, sententious, obese, with a cropped head and singularly wise eyes. These eyes were now regarding Molinari.

"Well, what's new, *amigo?*"

His voice was not excessively cordial, but Molinari knew that visitors did not displease him. Besides, Parodi's possible reaction was of less importance to him than the need of finding a confidant and advisor. Slowly and efficaciously, Parodi was sipping maté from a little blue jug. He offered it to Molinari. The latter, although impatient to explain the irrevocable adventure that had disarranged his life, knew that it was useless to try to hurry Isidro Parodi. With a tranquility that surprised him, he initiated a trivial dialogue touching on horse racing, which is a pure

66

racket, since no one knows who is going to win. Don Isidro paid no attention to him and returned to his preferred state of animosity. He expressed his opposition to the Italians, who had infiltrated everywhere, without respect even for the National Penitentiary.

"It is now full of foreigners of the most questionable background and no one knows where they're coming from."

Molinari, nationalistic without effort, agreed with this complaint and said that he was fed up with Italians and Druses, not to mention the English capitalists who had filled the country with railroads and refrigerators. Only yesterday he had entered the Los Hinchas Pizzeria and the first person he had seen was an Italian.

"Is it a male or female Italian that's gotten you so upset?"

"Neither," said Molinari simply. "*Don* Isidro, I have killed a man."

"They say I killed one, too, but nevertheless here I am. Don't get distraught. That Druse business is complicated, but if some clerk from the Eighteenth Precinct doesn't step into it, perhaps we can save your skin."

Molinari looked at him in amazement. Then he remembered that his name had been linked to the mystery of Abenjaldún's villa by an unscrupulous daily—very different, to be sure, from the dynamic Cordone paper for which he wrote up the gentle sports and soccer. He remembered that Parodi retained his mental agility and that, thanks to his ardor and the generous distraction of Deputy Inspector Grondona, he submitted the afternoon papers to a lucid examination. As a matter of fact, *don* Isidro was well aware of the recent disappearance of Abenjaldún. However, he asked Molinari to recount the facts to him, but not to speak too rapidly because he was now partly deaf in one ear. Molinari, almost serene now, related the story:

"Believe me, I am a modern fellow, a man of my times. I have lived, but I also like to meditate. I understand that we have now overcome the era of materialism; the communions and the agglomerations of people from the Eucharistic Congress have left an irradicable mark on me. As you were saying last time—

67

and, believe me, the comment didn't fall unnoticed—we must clear up the unknown. You know, the fakirs and yogis, with all their respiratory exercises and that nonsense, do know a few things. I, as a good Catholic, renounced the Honor and Country Spiritual Group; but I have heard that the Druses are a progressive collective society and that they are nearer the mystery than most people who go to Mass on Sundays. Anyway, Dr. Abenjaldún had a sumptuous villa in Villa Mazzini with a phenomenal library. I met him at Radio Fenix, on Arbor Day. He gave a very clever speech, and he liked a little article of mine that a friend had given him.

"He took me to his house, lent me some serious books, and invited me to parties that he gave at the villa. The female element was lacking, but these were cultural gatherings. I assure you. Some people say that they believe in pagan gods, but in the meeting room there is a metal bull that's worth more than a streetcar. Every Friday, around the bull gather the *akils,* who are, you might say, the initiates. For some time Dr. Abenjaldún had been wanting me to become one of these. I couldn't refuse: it was advisable for me to be in good with the old fellow, and a man doesn't live on bread alone.

"The Druses are a very closed group and some of them didn't feel that an Occidental was worthy of entering their brotherhood. In short, Abul Hasán, the owner of the fleet of meat transport trucks, had pointed out that the number of persons chosen is fixed and that it is not permitted to make conversions. The treasurer Izedín also was opposed. But he's a wretch who spends all day writing and Dr. Abenjaldún used to laugh at him and his books. Nevertheless, these reactionaries with their antiquated prejudices continued their undermining work, and I don't hesitate to say that, indirectly, they are at fault for everything.

"On the eleventh of August I received a letter from Abenjaldún, stating that on the fourteenth I would be subjected to a rather difficult trial for which I had to prepare myself."

"How did you have to prepare yourself?" inquired Parodi.

"Well, you know, three days on tea alone, learning the signs of the zodiac in order as they are found in the Bristol Almanac.

68

I phoned in sick at the Sanitary Works where I work in the mornings. At first, I was surprised that the ceremony was scheduled for a Sunday and not a Friday, but the letter explained that for so important an examination the Lord's Day was more suitable. I was to appear at the villa before midnight. Friday and Saturday I spent in the most peaceful fashion, but Sunday I awoke nervous. You know, *don* Isidro, now that I think about it, I'm sure I had a presentiment about what was going to happen. But I didn't falter, and I spent the whole day with the book. It was funny—I would glance at the clock every five minutes to see if I could have another glass of tea yet. With all this waiting I still got to Retiro late and I had to take the 11:18 train instead of the earlier one.

"Even though I was thoroughly prepared, I kept studying the Almanac on the way. I was distracted by a couple of fools who were discussing the victory of the Millionaires over the Chacarita Juniors and, take my word, they didn't know beans about soccer. I got off at Belgrano R. The villa is thirteen blocks from the car stop. I figured that the walk would refresh me, but it left me half dead. Following Abenjaldún's instructions, I phoned him from the grocery on Rosetti Street.

"In front of the villa there was a line of parked cars. The house had more lights burning than a wake, and even from a distance you could hear the murmur of the people. Abenjaldún was waiting for me inside the gate. He seemed somehow aged to me. I had seen him frequently, but only during the day. At that moment, I realized that he looked a little like Repetto, but with a beard. Life is strange, as they say: that evening, nearly out of my mind over the examination, and I am struck by that stupid thought.

"We went along the brick path that circles the house and entered at the rear. In the office was Izedín, standing near the filing room."

"I've been filed away for fourteen years," observed *don* Isidro pleasantly. "But I am unfamiliar with that filing room. Describe the layout a bit."

"Well, it's very simple. The office is on the upper floor; a

69

stairway leads down directly to the main meeting room. There below were the Druses, some one hundred and fifty in number, all covered from head to foot by white tunics, standing about the metal bull. The filing room is a little cubicle situated off the office, a sort of interior room. I always say that an enclosure without a window is inevitably unhealthy. Don't you think so?"

"Don't speak to me about that. Since I settled down here in the north, I've grown sick and tired of enclosures. Describe the office to me."

"It's a large room. There's an oak desk with an Olivetti on it, several very comfortable armchairs into which you sink clear up to your neck, an ancient Turkish hookah worth a small fortune, a tasseled chandelier, a futuristic Persian rug, a bust of Napoleon, a library of scholarly works—*La Historia Universal de César Cantú, Las Maravillas del Mundo y del Hombre, La Biblioteca Internacional de Obras Famosas, El Anuario de la Razon, El Tesoro de la Juventud,* by Peluffo, *La Donna Delincuente,* by Lombardo, and Lord knows what else.

"Izedín was nervous. I discerned immediately why. He had apparently been pressing Abenjaldún to read over some of his writings. On the table was a huge package of books. Abenjaldún, more interested in my examination, wanted to get rid of Izedín and he told him: 'Don't worry. I'll read your books tonight.'

"I have no idea whether the other man believed him. He went to put on his tunic in order to go down to the main meeting room. He didn't even glance at me.

"As soon as we were alone, Dr. Abenjaldún said, 'Have you fasted religiously, have you learned the twelve signs of the zodiac?'

"I assured him that since Thursday evening at ten o'clock (that evening, in the company of a few high priests of the new sensibility, I had dined on mild Italian sausage and baked fish at the Mercado de Abasto) I had been on tea alone. Abenjaldún asked me to recite the names of the twelve figures. I did so without a single error, and he made me repeat the list five or six times. Finally he said, 'I see that you have taken your instructions seriously. This, however, would avail you nothing if you

70

weren't industrious and valiant. I am satisfied that you possess these qualities, and I have resolved to ignore those who deny your capacity. I shall subject you to a single trial—the loneliest and most difficult one. Thirty years ago, in the peaks of Lebanon, I executed it felicitously. But beforehand the masters had subjected me to easier trials: I found a coin at the bottom of the sea; a jungle made of air; a calyx in the center of the earth, a cutlass condemned to Hell. You shall not search for four magic objects; you shall seek the four masters who form the veiled tetragon of the Divinity. Now, engaged in pious tasks, they are gathered about the metal bull. They are praying with their brothers, the *akils,* veiled just as they are. Nothing distinguishes them, but your heart will recognize them. I shall order you to bring Yusuf. You will go down into the meeting room, envisioning in their precise order the figures of Heaven; when you arrive at the last figure, that of Pisces, you will return to the first, which is Aries, and thus repeatedly. You will circle three times about the *akils,* and your steps will bring you to Yusuf— if you have not altered the order of the figures. You will say, "Abenjaldún calls you," and you will bring him here. Then I shall order you to bring the second master, then the third, and, finally, the fourth.'

"Fortunately, from having read and reread the Bristol Almanac so much, the twelve figures were engraved in my mind. But all it takes is for someone to tell you not to make a mistake to make you start worrying about erring. I wasn't daunted, I assure you, but I had a presentiment. Abenjaldún shook my hand, told me that his prayers went with me, and I then headed down the stairway that leads to the meeting room. I was all absorbed in the signs. Besides, those white figures, those bowed heads, those blank faces, and that sacred bull had me upset. Nevertheless, I circled the group three times in the proper fashion and found myself behind a sheet-covered figure who looked to be the same as all the others. But, since I was envisioning the zodiac signs, I had no time to think, and I said to him, 'Abenjaldún calls you.' The man followed me. While I continued imagining the signs we went up the stairway and entered the

71

office. Abenjaldún was praying. He had Yusuf go with him into the filing room, and almost immediately he returned and said to me, 'Now bring Ibrahim.'

"I went downstairs, covered my three laps, stopped behind another sheet-covered figure, and said, 'Abenjaldún calls you.' I returned with him to the office."

"Hold your horses," said Parodi. "Are you sure that while you were circling about downstairs no one left the office?"

"I swear, I'm sure no one did. I was very attentive to the signs and all the rest, but I'm not that dumb. I never took my eye off that door. Don't worry. No one entered or left.

"Abenjaldún took Ibrahim by the arm and led him into the filing room. Then he said to me, 'Now bring Izedín.' It was strange, *don* Isidro, the first two times I was sure of myself. This time I lost my nerve. I went down, circled the Druses three times, and returned with Izedín. I was thoroughly fatigued: on the stairway my vision clouded over—kidney trouble, you know. Everything seemed strange to me, even my companion. Abenjaldún, who now had so much faith in me that instead of praying was playing solitaire, took Izedín to the filing room and said to me, in a fatherly tone, 'This exercise has worn you out. I shall seek the fourth initiate, who is Jalil.'

"Fatigue is the enemy of attention, but as soon as he left I hung onto the bars of the balcony and watched him carefully. The man calmly made the three tours, grabbed Jalil by the arm, and brought him upstairs. I've already told you that the only door to the filing room is the one that opens into the office. Through that door went Abenjaldún with Jalil, and shortly he emerged with the four veiled Druses. He made the sign of the cross over me—since they are a very devout people; then he told them in our language to take off their head coverings. You won't believe it, but there were Izedín, with his foreigner's face, and Jalil, the assistant manager of La Formal, and Yusuf, the brother-in-law of that chap who talks through his nose, and Ibrahim, as white as death with his long beard—Abenjaldún's partner, you know. One hundred and fifty identical Druses—and here were the four masters!

"Dr. Abenjaldún nearly embraced me. But the others, who are persons little impressed by evidence and full of superstitions and auguries, didn't offer a single palm to clasp and began grumbling at Abenjaldún in Druse. Poor Abenjaldún tried to convince them, but finally he had to give in. He said that he would submit me to another trial, an extremely difficult one. But in the balance of this trial would hang the lives of all of them, and perhaps even the fate of the world. He continued:

" 'We shall cover your eyes with this veil and we shall place in your right hand this long cane. Each of us will hide in some corner of the house or the gardens. You shall wait here until the clock strikes twelve; then you will find us successively, guided by the figures. These signs rule the world. During your examination we shall trust in you for the order of the figures: the cosmos will be in your power. If you do not change the order of the zodiac, our destinies and the destiny of the world will continue along their prefixed course. If your memory fails, if after Libra you imagine Leo and not Scorpio, the master whom you seek will perish and the world will know the menace of air, of water, and of fire.'

"All agreed except Izedín, who had consumed so much salami that his eyelids were growing heavy and who was so absentminded that on departing he shook the hands of all of us—something which he never does.

"They gave me the bamboo cane, placed the blindfold over my eyes, and left. I was alone. You can't imagine how tense I felt! Going over the figures without changing the order; waiting for the bells which never seemed to sound; afraid that they would sound and I would begin to move through that house that suddenly seemed interminable and unknown to me. Without wanting to I thought of the stairway, the descents, the furniture that there would be in my path, of the cellar, the patio, the skylight, Lord knows what all. I began to hear all sorts of noises: the branches of the trees in the garden, steps above my head, the Druses who were leaving the villa, the starter on the old Isetta of Abd-el-Meleh—you know, the one who won the Raggio Oil raffle.

73

"Finally, everyone had gone and I was alone in that massive house with the Druses hidden Heaven knows where. So, when the clock struck twelve I was startled. I moved out with my cane—I, a young chap, bursting with life, staggering like an invalid, like a blind man, if you get my point. I moved towards the left, because the brother-in-law of that fellow who talks through his nose has quite a bit of *savoir-faire* and I figured that I'd find him under the desk. All the while I was seeing clearly Libra, Scorpio, Sagittarius, and all those designs. I forgot the first landing in the stairway and kept descending while on the level. Afterward, I entered the winter garden. And suddenly I was lost. I could find neither doors nor walls. By the way, keep this in mind: three straight days on tea alone and the great mental expenditure demanded of me. In spite of everything, I dominated the situation and moved along beside the serving table.

"I suspected that one of them might have climbed into the coalbin, but these Druses, as learned as they might be, lack our native acuteness. From there I headed back towards the meeting room, where I ran into a three-legged table of the kind used by some Druses who believe in spiritualism, as if they were still in the Middle Ages. I had a feeling that all the eyes of the oil paintings on the walls were staring at me. You'll laugh, perhaps, but my sister always says I have something of a madman and a poet about me. But anyway, I didn't relent, and suddenly I discovered Abenjaldún. I just reached out my arm and there he was. Without too much trouble we found the stairway—which was much closer than I had imagined—and we reached the office. On the way we exchanged not a word. I was busy with the figures. I left him there and went in search of another Druse. At that moment I heard something that sounded like a stifled laugh. Immediately afterward, I heard a cry. I would swear that I didn't make a mistake with the zodiac signs—but first with my anger, and then with the surprise, perhaps I had erred. I'm not one to deny the evidence. I turned around and, tapping along with my cane, I re-entered the office. I stumbled over something on the floor. I bent over

74

and touched hair with my hand. I felt a nose, and eyes. Without realizing what I was doing, I tore off the blindfold.

"Abenjaldún was stretched out on the carpet—his mouth was frothy with blood. I touched him; he was still warm, but he was already dead. There wasn't a soul in the room. I spied the cane that had fallen from my hand. There was blood on the tip. In that instant I realized that I had killed him. Doubtless, when I heard the laugh and the cry, I had become momentarily confused and changed the order of the figures. That confusion has cost the life of a man. Perhaps those of the four masters, too.

"I went to the balcony and called to them. No one answered. Terrified, I fled through the back of the house, repeating under my breath, 'Aries, Taurus, Gemini,' to keep the world from collapsing. Suddenly I came to the back wall that runs for three quarters of a block along the street. Tullido Ferrarotti always said my future was in the middle-distance races. But that night I was a marvel at the high jump. In one leap I scaled the wall, which is a good six feet high. While I was picking myself up from the gutter and removing some of the bits of broken glass that were incrusted everywhere on me, I began to cough from the smoke. From the villa was coming a cloud of black smoke as thick as mattress wool. Even though I wasn't in training, I ran as I did in the old days. When I arrived at Rosetti, I looked back. There was a light in the sky like the twenty-fifth of May —the house was afire. That goes to show you what a change in the order of the figures can do!

"Just thinking about it made my mouth dryer than a parrot's tongue. I spotted a policeman on the corner and I turned back. Then I got into some desolate spot that it's a pity to find still in the capital. I was suffering like a good man, let me tell you, and a couple of dogs had me out of my mind. It only takes one of them to start barking to set off a whole pack of them deafening you from a few feet away. And in those eastern suburbs there's no safety for the pedestrian, no police vigilance of any kind. Quickly I calmed down because by then I had reached Charlone Street. I made a few turns and I found myself before the walls of the Chacarita Cemetery, A gang of hoodlums hanging about a grocery store began to chant 'Aries, Leo,' and made noises that sound badly in one's mouth. But I paid no attention to them and went on.

"Would you believe that only some time later did I realize that I had been repeating the signs—out loud? I proceeded to get lost again. You are aware that in those suburbs they are ignorant of the rudiments of urbanism and the streets are lost in a veritable labyrinth. It never occurred to me to take a cab. I arrived home with my shoes an absolute mess at the moment when the garbage collectors come calling. That dawn I was dead tired. I think I even had a temperature. I stretched out on the bed but resolved not to sleep—in order not to lose track of the figures.

"At noon I called in sick at the newspaper and at the Sanitary Works. At that moment my neighbor, the traveling salesman for Brancato, came in and insisted that I accompany him to his room for a spaghetti feast. I'm speaking to you seriously now. At first I felt a little better. My friend is a pleasantly worldly chap, and he opened a bottle of domestic muscatel. But I was in no mood for fine conversation and, taking advantage of the fact that the spaghetti sauce had settled in my stomach like a ball of lead, I went to my room. I didn't go out all day. Nevertheless, since I'm no hermit and since the business of the night before had me upset, I asked the landlady to bring me a copy of *Noticias*. Without even glancing at the sports page, I dived into the police news and spied the picture of the disaster: At 12:23 a fire of vast proportions had broken out in the residence-villa of Dr. Abenjaldún, located in Villa Mazzini. In spite of the praiseworthy intervention by the fire department, the dwelling was razed by the flames, with the owner, Dr. Abenjaldún, one of the great pioneers in the importing of linoleum substitutes, perishing in the blaze. I was terrified.

"Baudizzoni, who always was careless with his pages, had committed a few errors. For example, he hadn't made the slightest mention of the religious ceremony and had stated that that night they had met in order to read the minutes and elect new officers. A short while before the occurrence, Messrs.

Jahil, Yusuf, and Ibrahim had left the villa. These individuals declared that until midnight they had been chatting with the deceased, who, far from sensing the tragedy that would end his days and reduce to ashes one of the traditional west-end residences, was glorying in his customary high spirits. The origin of the great conflagration was yet to be determined.

"I'm not a man afraid of work, but since that day I haven't returned to the newspaper or to the Works, and my spirits are dragging on the ground. A few days after all this a very affable gentleman came to see me. He questioned me regarding my role in the purchase of brooms and cleaning rags for the bar frequented by the workers at the stockyard on Bucarelli Street. Afterwards he changed the subject and spoke of the foreign collective groups and referred specifically to the Sirio-Lebanese society. He promised, in a vague manner, to call again. But he did not return. Rather, a strange man stationed himself on the corner and now follows me with a great show of secrecy wherever I go. I am aware that you are a man who doesn't allow himself to get tangled up with the police or anyone else. So please save me, *don* Isidro. I'm at my wits' end!"

"I'm no sorcerer or faster to be going around solving riddles. But I won't deny you a bit of a helping hand. However, understand, on one condition. Promise me you'll do just as I say."

"Whatever you wish, *don* Isidro."

"All right. Let's begin right away. Give the figures from the Almanac in their correct order."

"Aries, Taurus, Gemini, Cancer, Leo, Virgo, Libra, Scorpio, Sagittarius, Capricorn, Aquarius, Pisces."

"Good. Now say them backwards."

Molinari, paling, stammered:

"Sarie, Saurut, Imineg . . ."

"Stop that foolishness. I said change the order, give them in any order at all."

"Any order at all? You didn't understand, *don* Isidro. You can't do that . . ."

"Oh no? Say the first one, the last one, and the fifth one."

Molinari, terrified, complied. Then he looked about him.

"Okay, now that you've gotten these fantasies out of your head, go to the newspaper. And stop stewing over all this."

Silent, liberated, bewildered, Molinari left the cell. Outside, the other man was waiting for him.

II

A week later Molinari admitted that he could no longer put off a second visit to the Penitentiary. Nonetheless, it bothered him to think of facing Parodi, who had penetrated his presumption and miserable incredulity. A man of the times, like him, allowing himself to be tricked by a bunch of fanatic foreigners! The appearances of the affable man were becoming more frequent and more sinister. They no longer talked only of the Sirio-Lebanese but also of the Druses of Lebanon. The visitor's dialogue had become enriched with new topics: for example, the abolition of torture in 1813, the advantages of an electric coaxer imported from Bremen by the Department of Investigations, and so on.

One rainy morning Molinari took the bus from the corner of Humberto I. When he got off at Palermo, the stranger, who had passed from dark glasses to a red beard, got off too . . .

Parodi, as always, received him with a certain gruffness. He had the tact not to allude to the Villa Mazzini mystery. Rather, he spoke—as was common with him—of what can be done by a man with a thorough knowledge of a deck of cards. He evoked the memory of Lince Rivarola who caught a blow from a chair at the very moment when he was extracting a second ace of spades from a special device he had in his sleeve. In order to illustrate the anecdote he took from a drawer a greasy deck of cards, had Molinari shuffle it, and asked him to spread the cards out on the table face down. He said:

"My good friend, you who are a wizard are going to give this poor old man the four of hearts."

Molinari stammered:

"I've never pretended to be a wizard, *señor* . . . You must know that I've broken off all contact with those fanatics . . ."

"You have cut and shuffled; now give me this minute the four of hearts. Don't be afraid; it will be the first card you pick up."

Trembling, Molinari reached out his hand, took the first card he encountered, and gave it to Parodi. The latter looked at him and said:

"You're a real wonder. Now you'll give me the jack of spades."

Molinari picked out another card and gave it to Parodi.

"Now the seven of clubs."

Molinari gave him a card.

"This exercise has tired you out. I'll pick out the last card for you, which will be the king of hearts."

He picked up, almost recklessly, a card and added it to the three others. Then he told Molinari to turn them over. They were the king of hearts, the seven of clubs, the jack of spades, and the four of hearts.

"Don't sit there with your eyes popping out," said Parodi. "Among all these cards there's one that's marked—that's the one I asked you for first, but it wasn't the first one you gave me. I asked you for the jack of spades, and you gave me the seven of clubs. I asked you for the seven of clubs, and you gave me the king of hearts. I said that you were tired and that I myself would pick out the last card, the king of hearts. I picked up the four of hearts, which has the little black spots on it.

"Abenjaldún did the same. He told you to get Druse Number 1, you brought him Number 2; he told you to bring Number 2, you brought Number 3; he told you to bring Number 3, and you brought Number 4; he told you that he was going to get Number 4, and he brought Number 1. Number 1 was Ibrahim, his intimate friend. Abenjaldún could spot him in a group of the others . . . This is what happens when you get mixed up with foreigners. You yourself told me that the Druses were a very closed group. You said a mouthful. And the most secretive of them all was Abenjaldún, the senior member of the

79

society. For the others it was enough to rebuff a naturalized Argentine; he wanted to make a big joke of it all.

"He told you to come on Sunday, and you yourself told me that Friday was their ceremonial day. In order to set your nerves on edge he kept you for three days on straight tea and Bristol Almanac. On top of it all, he made you walk I don't know how many blocks. He set you loose in the midst of a ceremony of sheeted Druses and, as if that much fear weren't enough to confuse you, he invented that business about the signs in the Almanac. He was in a rare mood for joking.

"He had not yet examined (nor will he ever examine) Izedín's accounting books. It was about those books that they were talking when you arrived. You imagined that they were discussing novels and poetry. No one will ever know what juggling the treasurer had done with his accounts. What *is* evident is that he killed Abenjaldún and burned the house down so that no one would ever see the books. He took leave of you, and shook your hand—a thing which he never does—in order to give the impression that he had left. He hid nearby, waited for the others, who had had enough of the joke, to go, and when you with your cane and blindfold were looking for Abenjaldún, he returned to the office. When you came back with the old fellow, the two of them had to laugh at you groping about like a blind man. You left to find him once more and make four trips back, in your groping fashion, always escorting the same man.

"At that moment the treasurer stabbed him in the back. You heard his cry. While you were feeling your way back to the room, Izedín hurried off and burned up the books. Then, in order to justify the disappearance of the accounts, he set fire to the house."

PIROPOS AT MIDNIGHT
Antonio Helú

Antonio Helú is the dean of Mexican detective fiction authors. As far back as the twenties he was publishing crime stories in Mexico City. His principal contribution to date has been the volume of short stories The Obligation to Kill *(1946), which traces the criminal and sleuthing career of Helú's inimitable Máximo Roldán. Roldán does indeed act at times as a detective, but the reader needs to be let in on the secret that his last name is an anagram of the Spanish word "ladrón" (thief) and that his full name would thus come out in English as Supreme Crook. Helú's literary model is Maurice Leblanc's celebrated rogue-detective, Arsène Lupin; but, at the same time, this sort of extra-legal toying with the machinery of justice reflects the characteristic Mexican attitude of skepticism towards the forces of law. Mexican sympathies often go out instinctively to a criminal if his crime involves a clear-cut conflict between freedom of individual expression and abstract (and thus remote) justice. "Piropos at Midnight," taken from* The Obligation to Kill, *demonstrates quite neatly how our Latin friend Roldán operates.*

Piropos at Midnight
ANTONIO HELÚ

"TOOTLE-LOO, *sweetheart!*"

Máximo Roldán turned in his tracks, astonished. A *piropo**— in open violation of the law? The author of the comment must have been hopelessly insane to expose himself in this way to imprisonment. Roldán looked this way and that without discovering anyone nearby. Nonetheless, he had not been mistaken. The *piropo* had been pronounced no more than a few feet away. Yet the only person in sight was the police officer on duty at the corner up ahead.

Máximo Roldán continued on, and two steps further along: "*What inviting eyes!*"

This time the *piropo* was articulated in a louder tone, with all the enthusiasm that the expression required. Even the policeman at the corner couldn't have failed to hear it. And he didn't fail to hear it. Máximo Roldán realized that he was picking up his lantern and approaching him with slow steps.

The next thing heard was:

"*What a graceful walk!*"

The policeman reached Máximo Roldán and lifted his lantern to head level.

"Who are you saying these things to?"

"Me? To no one."

The policeman looked all about him. His scrutiny covered

---

* A "piropo" is a spontaneous oral compliment, traditionally offered by Latin men to females passing by in the street. They may range from poetry to vulgarity. At one time the public uttering of "piropos" was prohibited by law in Mexico City.

83

the entire length of the street, from one sidewalk to the other, and only on down the street, about a hundred yards away, could he discern any people.

Then it came again:

"*Ah, for just a single glimpse from your adorable eyes . . .*"

"Now, look here!" exclaimed the policeman indignantly. But immediately he became aware that the voice could not be that of Máximo Roldán. And now he looked behind him, in front of him, above him. No one. Not a window, not a balcony, not even a door was nearby. Even the rooftops were some thirty feet above them. And the *piropos*—or whatever they were— were clearly originating not more than a few feet away.

"Well! What do you make of this?" he said finally, bewildered, abandoning his visual search.

And, annoyed, he took his lantern, walked back to the corner, and resumed his post.

Then the situation changed somewhat. Instead of a *piropo*, out into the night air floated:

"*Hey, chief!*"

And since this allusion was unmistakably direct, the officer returned to where Roldán stood.

"Well," said the policeman. "It appears to me that . . ."

"It appears to me," interrupted Máximo Roldán, "that robbers are at work under your very nose, and you don't even realize it."

"Eh?"

"I said there's a robbery going on! Can't you hear? Take out your gun and follow me. Leave your lantern behind! The lan— tern! You'd scare them off, don't you see? Get rid of it and let's hurry. Don't worry, even if it's smashed to bits when you get back, leave it! That's right! Now, got your gun ready? Come on. Wait a minute, don't make so much noise! Quietly now."

They rounded the corner.

"Do you have your night stick?"

"Yes."

"Let me have it."

The policeman held out the club to Roldán. He was holding

the pistol before him with one hand, and was automatically complying with what the other man ordered.

"Keep pointing the gun straight ahead. Over this way, towards the window and the doorway. That's it. Careful now. Something's moving in the window. Quickly, they're leaving!"

The moment he had come around the corner, Roldán saw the nearby window and the door which the building lacked on the other side. Two men were now slipping out of the window, trying to reach the ground with their dangling toes. At that same moment, scarcely a yard away, the door opened and another man appeared, coming out of the doorway backwards struggling with some bulky object he was carrying.

In a flash, Roldán was beneath the window, and the policeman was standing near the door.

"Tell them to put up their hands. If they try to escape, shoot. That's it. Good and high. And you there, friend, drop that bundle on the ground. There we are. Now up with your hands. Come over this way a little more. Over here with your friends."

The three men, with their arms raised, lined up in a row before Roldán. "Got them covered?" he asked.

"Right."

"If they make a move, you'll fire, eh?"

"That's right."

"Excellent. Now I'll search them."

Roldán went over to the robbers and began a thorough search of one after the other. He turned all their pockets inside out, and minutely examined their clothing and their hats.

"*Caramba!* Haven't they got anything? You fellows must have lifted something . . . Well, let's see. Ah, in this bundle perhaps. But that scarcely seems possible. Put the money into a bundle with a load of other things . . . Other things, I say, because this can't all be money . . ."

It was at this precise moment when the second policeman appeared. Roldán, bending over the bundle lying near the door, heard a voice speak up from directly behind him:

"Can I help out here, friend?"

This was the first indication of the presence of the other

85

policeman. Of the *other* policeman, since Roldán's first companion remained mute, his revolver trained on the three criminals, unmoved by any occurrence. He was the perfect incarnation of the iron-nerved man to whom nothing comes as a surprise.

There was a moment of thunderous silence, which Roldán finally shattered.

"*Hombre!* You must have been dropped right out of heaven . . . Help me? Are you serious? Help with what? Don't you see that there are only three of them? And my partner, see how he's got them all in the sights of his gun? Why he alone could handle the whole bunch. But, if you wish . . . or, wait a minute. Look here. I'll have to go into the building again to see if there's anyone else in there. Do you have a gun? You do? Let me have it. Just for a minute, a few seconds, while I skip in and right back out."

Roldán had gradually been approaching as he talked, and he held out his hand to receive the pistol. The other fellow scarcely had time to make a move to refuse him, since Roldán's hand had already closed around the gun butt and, giving a jerk, he pulled the weapon out of its holster.

"There we are," continued the determined chatterer. "Now who was it who lugged this bundle out? . . . What muscles you must have, friend. I congratulate you. All right now. Partner?"

"What is it?"

"Before I go into the building, I want to explain something to you. Are you listening?"

"Sure."

"Very good. But listen very carefully to what I say. It could be very serious if you missed what I'm going to tell you."

"Don't worry, sir."

"Okay. Do you remember the moment when we first heard the *piropos?*"

"Yes."

"There wasn't anyone along the street who could have spoken to them, right?"

"Just you and I."

"But neither you nor I uttered them. And there weren't any doors or windows that they could have come from. So unless a miracle was taking place . . . Do you believe in miracles?"

"Do you, sir?"

"No."

"Well, I don't either."

"All right. Then it was not a question of a miracle. Nevertheless, the *piropos* could be heard near us. If there was, on the other hand, a thing nearby . . . Do you remember what thing was near us?"

"No, sir."

"Don't you remember what you placed your lantern on?"

"My lantern?"

"Yes. On top of what did you leave the lantern?"

"Well—sir, on top of—of—on top of the garbage can."

"And inside the garbage can a man may fit perfectly well. That was where the voice came from. A hole cut in the side of the can allowed his voice to be heard quite clearly."

"*Caramba!* Why didn't we think of looking there?"

"Why should we have done that? The important thing to be understood was what the purpose was of the owner of that voice. It was heard too clearly, too loud, too strong and sure to have belonged to a man in a drunken condition. Now then, I was the only person passing by that spot. I hesitated to accept that the *piropos* were directed to me. And the only other person who could possibly have heard them was you. Therefore, not being directed at me, they were intended for you."

"For me?" exclaimed the policeman with not a little alarm.

"Don't get upset, friend. They were for you, but not because of the gracefulness of your walk. It was a question simply of getting your attention, distracting you, in short, of making you abandon your corner. When a disturbance breaks out in the street, it's your duty to intercede; and you have the same duty when you hear someone drop a *piropo* in the street. The purpose of the whole thing, then, began to become clear in my mind: it was an effort to lure you to a spot from which you would not have the same field of vision as at your post. Stationed near the garbage can, you could discern everything up and down that one street. On the other hand, there hidden from view was the street that passed in front, at right angles. It was only reasonable to assume that the dirty work was being carried out there."

"What dirty work, sir?"

"The robbery, my good chap! Don't you even understand what I'm saying to you?"

"Why, yes, of course. Continue."

"When at one moment you tried to return to your post, the voice cried, '*Hey, chief!*'"

"Yes, that's right."

"There's no longer any doubt in my mind that the object of the *piropos* was to lure you away and prevent your seeing what was happening on the street that was then out of sight to you. For that reason I deemed it fitting to say that there was a robbery going on under your very nose. And you can see now how right I was."

The policeman continued waving his gun towards the criminals. He was not, however, the only person hanging on Máximo Roldán's words. The other policeman and the three captives were also listening with great interest. "And now, my friend, remember that you left your lantern on top of the can? Well go and take a look . . . It's probably smashed to bits."

"Smashed—to bits?"

"Certainly. Do you think that the person inside was planning to stay there all his life? On raising the lid to get out, the lantern must have toppled to the ground. Go ahead and see. I'll wait here, that is, *we'll* wait here guarding these men. Why don't you leave me your pistol? That's fine, thanks."

The policeman handed over his revolver to Roldán, and hurried off to the corner. He arrived there, went around it quickly, and suddenly there was heard a cry of surprise, and the noise of footsteps that receded at a full run.

"I'm sorry," said Roldán, addressing the three men who were standing with their hands held high. "I'm afraid that if he catches up with your friend he'll settle accounts over the broken lantern . . . Well, that bundle stays here . . . You fellows can go . . .

Yes, I mean it . . . You can go . . . Take off . . . Straight down this street, without turning your heads. Hurry up, before the other policeman gets back . . ."

The three men didn't bother even to lower their arms, but started walking away, quickened their step, and finally broke into a run. In the meantime, Roldán had approached the other policeman.

"You're staying here, my friend. Or rather you're going with me . . . Come along."

He slipped his gun hand into his pocket and pressed it against the policeman's back.

"Come on. Just keep in mind that I've got this pistol nudging you. Any fast move and I'll shoot. Do I make myself clear? Good . . . Tell me now why you made the unfortunate move of appearing when you did. To save the bundle? You've seen how little it means to me. Perhaps you did it in the hope of rescuing your companions. In a policeman's uniform you can accomplish many things, to be sure. But you made a miscalculation. When a policeman arrives he is always accompanied by the loudest racket possible. And you showed up on the spot so quietly— as if you had been dropped from heaven. And I commented on that fact, eh—that you seemed to have dropped right out of the sky. But you see now, don't you, my friend, that neither the other policeman nor I believe in miracles. No, heaven doesn't drop down policemen; so that in order to have appeared as you did, you had to have come out of the open doorway. And as far as I was concerned, everyone who came stealthily out of that doorway was a criminal. So you see that not for even a minute did you fool me into thinking that you were anything but a robber disguised as a policeman."

The two were strolling along in the most natural of fashions. The man who walked with Roldán, having completely forgotten his situation, was carefully taking in the things he was hearing. He ventured to speak:

"*Diablo!* People like you, on the police force, are going to give us nothing but trouble!"

"My good fellow! Who told you I was on the police force?

On the contrary! On the contrary! Possibly you didn't see how I allowed your friends to escape. And didn't you notice how I arranged for the other policeman to go off unarmed, in order to save you all some trouble. A member of the police force! . . . *Vaya!* . . . But you'll see . . . When I determined that you, too, were a robber, I understood immediately why the others didn't have any money on them . . . This had seemed very strange to me: why should they have put the money, which was so easy to carry in one's pockets, into a big awkward bundle which was unwieldy and dangerous to boot. Only if they were a bunch of bumbling idiots would they have done a thing like that. Nevertheless, I started to have a look through the bundle, because I never doubted that besides the objects you were making off with in the bundle, you were coming away with money, too. So, I was just about to examine the contents of the bundle when you appeared—right out of the blue. Without a doubt a robber dressed as a policeman is the person one least suspects; and, for that reason, he is the one in whose hands stolen money is the safest. So now, will you please give me the money."

From this moment on the other man appeared aroused from his dreams. The first sign was a shudder that ran the length of his body. Then he turned to Máximo Roldán and regarded him for a moment. Finally, he said:

"Do you actually believe that I'm going to hand over the money to you? Now that's the limit!"

"I think you're forgetting that I have a gun pointed at you," replied Roldán quickly. "And it's a rather important thing to forget. It would be no trouble at all for me to squeeze the trigger . . . I wouldn't even be held for it . . . An astute policeman and I capture a band of robbers, and as they try to escape, I fire a shot wounding, or killing one of them—the leader, perhaps. It would be very easy to explain. And it goes without saying that it would be equally effortless for me to take over the money so that I may conveniently disappear and you may go off to wherever you wish? Doesn't this seem reasonable?"

The other man fought with himself for a brief instant, still undecided. Then, slowly, he indicated with his arm a spot on his breast and said:

"In this pocket are the bills; in my pants pockets you'll find gold."

"Much obliged," declared Máximo Roldán. "And now I shall issue you a receipt which you may show to your companions. Write the following: 'Received from *señor*—put your name in there—all the proceeds obtained in this evening's undertaking.' Now the date, and right below it—my signature."

THE PUZZLE OF THE BROKEN WATCH
María Elvira Bermúdez

María Elvira Bermúdez, a lawyer employed in the Mexican Supreme Court, is the most prolific female detective fiction author in the Spanish-speaking world. She is a noted critic and has compiled The Best Mexican Detective Stories *(1955), the only anthology to date dedicated exclusively to Mexican detective literature. In contrast to compatriot Antonio Helú, señora Bermúdez's models are North American. Since Ellery Queen is the most immediately discernible influence on her writing, it is evident that she stands apart from Helú also in her respectful adherence to the traditional requirements of the "chess problem" type of detective story. "The Puzzle of the Broken Watch" is a particularly good illustration of* señora *Bermúdez's methods. A dedicated and effective feminist long before feminism came into vogue, María Elvira Bermúdez is one of the most interesting figures—and one of the very few women—to contribute to the development of Spanish American detective fiction.*

The Puzzle of the Broken Watch

M A R Í A E L V I R A B E R M Ú D E Z

COMFORTABLY reclining on his divan, he was absorbed in reading the short stories of Arkadio Averchenko. He smoked slowly, absently, the smile that appeared and reappeared on his lips causing him to forget his cigarette. Suddenly, a man somewhat younger than he entered the room. It was his good friend Miguel Prado, the lawyer.

"*Quiúbole!*" greeted the newcomer. "Are you busy now?"

"Very busy," replied Armando Zozaya.

"Very busy?" exclaimed Miguel. "If all you're doing is reading—"

"So you think one can't be busy with a book?"

"Well, I suppose so, but I have to talk with you." He took the book from Zozaya's hands and sat down before him. The latter gave a sigh of resignation and retrieved his book. He found his place, carefully folded over a corner of the page, and settled back to listen to his friend.

"I'm defending a person who's charged with murder," explained Prado. "And I'm convinced of his innocence. The problem is I haven't been able to find a way to prove it. That's why I—came to see you."

"What is it that you want me to do?"

"Well, it's clear to me that the only way to get my client acquitted is to find the real murderer."

"Nicely put. But I question whether this is possible. You understand, of course, that it's one thing to find yourself at the scene of the crime, in possession of fresh facts, and another to investigate a crime committed Lord knows how long ago."

"Naturally. All the same, I think you can help me."

"I'll do what I can, Miguel. Go ahead and tell me what it's all about."

"My client, Juan García, is charged with having murdered his sister-in-law, an attractive young girl who lived with Juan and her married sister in the García home together with the couple's seven-year-old daughter. On the day in question, Rosa, the victim, stayed at home because of a bad cold, and she was left alone when her sister and the latter's daughter went out shopping. Juan, as usual, was at work, but unfortunately that day between eleven-thirty and noon he had left work without telling anyone where he was going. Juan's wife and daughter were at the market longer than usual. I think they went to get medicine for Rosa, or something of the sort. At any rate, what happened was that when they returned they found the girl dead. She had three bullet wounds in her chest. There were signs of a struggle. The murder weapon was found at the scene. It was a gun that belonged to my client."

"None of the neighbors heard the shots?"

"No. The murder occurred on the third of May, the day of Santa Cruz, which is celebrated by construction workers. There's a new building going up nearby, so it's very possible that the gunshots were taken for part of the racket made by the fireworks. What's more, these same circumstances explain why the neighbors, entertained by the festivities of the construction people, failed to observe closely who entered and left the girl's home."

"I see. And what does your client have to say about all this?"

"He didn't deny that he left work. Actually, he had to secure permission from his boss at the match factory to get time off. He claimed that he left work because he had received an anonymous message in which he was told to be at a spot near the factory at eleven-thirty. The place indicated was in Atlampa, there where Vallejo Street begins. The spot, you realize, is out of the way and usually deserted. The message he received insinuated that there was something of great importance he should know about the conduct of his wife. Juan's wife is a good soul, and never had he had cause for doubting her loyalty. But, as you can imagine, Juan was intrigued, then disturbed, and ended up

96

keeping the appointment. He couldn't have spent more than five minutes passing under the Nonoalco Bridge and covering the few blocks that separated him from Vallejo Street. He says he arrived precisely on time and waited half an hour, but that no one showed up to give him the slightest information on the matter suggested in the message. The only people he saw were a rag-picker and an old woman beggar, who were more than a little surprised when he asked them if they had called him. He was furious by this time and returned immediately to work. His obviously agitated manner which his fellow workers subsequently observed has since been interpreted as the nervousness to be expected in a man who has just committed a crime."

"How did the anonymous message come to him? Has he shown it to you?"

"Unfortunately, he tore it up when he realized he had been the victim of a cruel joke. The message had been delivered into his hands that same day when he arrived at work by a small boy who had said merely, 'A gentleman sends you this.' "

"Haven't they been able to find the lad?"

"Impossible. The authorities maintain that the boy doesn't exist, that he's a product of my client's imagination, created in an attempt to establish an alibi for himself. And, as you know, I have neither the time nor the means to devote myself to the search for a little urchin lost in the streets of a city of four million people."

"Of course. Tell me, at what time has the murder been fixed?"

"Now that's the strangest thing in the whole case. Unquestionably, the murder had to have taken place during the period when Rosa's sister was absent—a space of two hours. However, according to a watch that belonged to the deceased, which was found in the possession of my client, the precise moment of the crime was eleven forty-five. The watch had been smashed, and the hands had stopped at that time."

"Very strange, very strange." Armando meditated a moment. Then he pursued the point. "I accept the fact that the smashing of the watch during the struggle that took place would leave the hands indicating the time of the victim's death, but what I don't

97

understand is why Juan, if he killed the girl, carried off the watch and kept it on his person."

"That's precisely what bothers me. What you might expect is that he would change the time indicated if he happened to notice it. Or that he'd leave it behind, not considering it a piece of evidence that could incriminate him. The District Attorney proposes that Juan carried it away and later lost his wits and forgot to get rid of it."

"That could be, but I don't believe so. For the time being we can arrive at the following conclusion: the fact that the day of Santa Cruz was selected for the crime so that the reports of the gun would be lost amid the noise of the fireworks, the delivery of the anonymous note to Juan with the object of strengthening his guilt through his absence from work, and, above all, the puzzling detail of that watch, strongly suggest that we are faced with a premeditated crime. One other thing, Miguel. Had the girl bought the watch for herself?"

"I don't know. It didn't occur to me to ask about that."

"It's very important. And, too, why were the sister and her little girl gone so long on their errand?"

"Do you believe that this has something to do with the problem?"

"I don't think any detail should be overlooked."

"All right, then. Why don't we go and speak with the sister?"

"A very good idea," said Armando Zozaya. "I was about to suggest the same thing to you."

The tenement house where Juan's wife and daughter lived was one of the many tenements which characterized the older, poorer Mexico. It was located on Venus Street, near the highway to Laredo, in the heart of the Atlampa quarter. The grayish brick walls, ravaged by the years, opened onto a long, narrow entrance hall which greedily imprisoned the daylight. In the broad, open patio the light regained its freedom and joyfully poured down on the cracked paving tiles and glimmering pools. Blocking the path before them were countless little children, somber pigeons, and drying clothes scattered about like so many gay pennants. Against the walls, geraniums and rue, daisies and a carnation here and there emerged from the flower pots placed along the stairways and lay claim to a place in the sun. Armando and his friend entered the courtyard of the tenement house escorted by a dozen curious glances. Lupe, Juan's wife, lived in number 19. She came to the door in response to the lawyer's knock, and when she recognized the man who was defending her husband she politely invited them to come in.

The home consisted of a kitchen and two rooms, the smallest of which was crowded with tables, assorted junk, several un-painted pine chairs, and a number of earthenware utensils. The other room, which was a little larger, was divided into two parts by an improvised partition of bedspreads and sarapes. On one side was the couple's double bed and the child's crib, and on the other a cot and a small dressing table that had apparently be-longed to the deceased Rosa. Still hanging on the wall were the girl's clothes, in the corner was a wooden trunk, and placed about the room were religious images together with pictures torn from old calendars, all of which had represented the girl's worldly belongings. Lupe explained:

"This is where poor Rosa slept. I haven't been able yet to make myself pack up her things. I just can't believe that she's gone." And she dried a pious tear with her apron. She was about to add something more when she became aware of the sudden appearance of her daughter.

"Rosita," she ordered, "go out and play in the patio. Go on now, *ándale!*"

The child went out slowly, making a sad face. The mother added:

"I've told her that her father and Aunt Rosa have gone away on a trip, poor thing. She adored my sister. She was her god-mother."

The two visitors took seats around a humble table. Lawyer Prado explained to Lupe that *señor* Zozaya who accompanied him wanted to help in his defense of Juan and that he needed to know certain facts. Lupe said she was more than willing to tell him everything that she knew, but first she declared:

"God knows my Juan is a good man. I'm not saying that he didn't drink a little, or didn't—stray occasionally, like all men. But as far as what they say about him and my sister . . . that's pure lies. Neither my poor sister—may God bless her—nor Juan were capable of doing anything that—that would reflect on my honor, or that of my little girl. They are also whispering behind my back that Juan may have killed her because she failed to respond to his attentions. But I know that can't be true."

"Who do you think might have done it?" asked Armando.

"I don't know. Only God can say. Perhaps someone who broke in intending to steal something."

"Did you find any things missing?"

"No. They might have carried off the radio. It's the only object of value. But no, it wasn't touched."

"Haven't you considered that it might have been someone who knew Rosa who . . . who committed the crime?"

"Well, I just don't know." And she looked oddly at the lawyer.

"What just occurred to you, *señora?*" asked Armando. "Tell me what it is."

"Well . . . you see. Oh, God forgive me, but—"

"Go ahead. There's nothing to fear."

"Well . . . Rosa had a boy friend, you understand. And recently they had been quarreling. The neighbors wouldn't tell me anything, but the other day I'm sure I heard *doña* Chona, the woman from number 10, tell Tula, who lives in 5, that she'd seen Tomás come here that day."

"Tomás was Rosa's boy friend?"

"Yes. I asked Tula what *doña* Chona had told her, but she refused to tell me. They are very close, you know. When it comes to gossip they're unbeatable, but—"

"When it comes to giving help in something like this," interposed Miguel, "they're worthless. I haven't been able to get a word out of them either. I forgot to tell you, Armando, that the *señora* had told me about this before. I tried to make the women understand what was at stake, but they flatly refused to go and

100

testify in court. And if I ask that they be subpoenaed, I run the risk of making things worse. You understand."

"Uh huh. But we must keep this point in mind," commented Armando. And he added, "Tell me, *señora*, why were you longer than usual at the market that day?"

Lupe responded to the question with surprise. It was evident that she hadn't been expecting it. She replied:

"I? Well . . . that is. I had to go and pick up a prescription for my daughter, and . . ."

"The pharmacy, is it far away?"

"No, it's just a little ways away, at the corner of Heroes and Neptuno."

"I understand that you left at ten o'clock and that you returned at twelve . . ."

Lupe was confused. For the moment she was saved from the, question by the appearance of her daughter.

"Mama, the men are here to talk with you about Rosa, aren't they?"

"*Muchachita esa!* Didn't I tell you to go out?"

"Let her be," intervened Zozaya. "Come here, little one. You love your Aunt Rosa a lot, don't you?"

"Oh, yes. She buys me lots of caramels. And I play with her. And I wear her clothes, too."

At this point, the child, bent on showing the visitors how she played with her aunt, disappeared into the other room and returned laden with clothing and trinkets. She put a kerchief on her head, explaining that this was the way her aunt wore it, she threw on a dress and dragged it about the room with genuine grace, as if she were a princess at a royal ball. She made several trips to and from the other room, exhibiting one gewgaw after the other. Zozaya observed her good-naturedly while Prado and the wife looked on without comprehending why Zozaya was interested in the child's treasures. The latter, in one of her trips from the other room, brought out the most cherished article— her aunt's watch. Zozaya examined it with interest and asked:

"Is this the watch that was found in your husband's possession?"

101

"Yes, it is," replied Lupe. "They say he had it with him. What I think is that he took it away with him that day to have it fixed because it's broken. But at the police station they don't believe me."

Armando looked fixedly at her and asked:

"Had Rosa spoken to you about having broken the watch?"

"No," the woman replied, dropping her glance. "But that must have been what happened."

Armando interpreted the woman's theory as a feeble effort to clear her husband of the guilt of the crime. He took the watch in his hands and examined it at length.

"How is it that you happen to have this, *señora?*"

Miguel explained:

"Although it actually ought to be included as part of the evidence in the case, the *señora* expressed a desire to keep it as a memento of her sister, and one of the members of the police force who is a close friend of the Garcías arranged to have it returned to them before the trial was over."

"How about that!" exclaimed Armando. "The history of this watch gets stranger by the minute!"

As Armando was speaking, the little girl came to his side and, shaking her head, regarded the timepiece very seriously. Suddenly she took it from Armando's hand, turned it about in every direction, and exclaimed emphatically:

"This isn't Aunt Rosa's watch!"

"What are you saying, child?" murmured her mother in astonishment.

"It isn't, it isn't, it isn't!" repeated the little one with conviction.

"How do you know it's not?" asked Zozaya gently.

"Because it doesn't have the little hole."

"What little hole?" asked the three members of her audience simultaneously.

"A little hole here," the child explained. "Aunt Rosa made one for me because when I wore it, it was too big." And she indicated, beyond the normal series of perforations on the watch band, the unmarked expanse of leather.

102

THE PUZZLE OF THE BROKEN WATCH

"A child's nonsense. Pay no attention to her," said Lupe.

"It's *not* the watch, it's *not* the watch," the little girl insisted.

Her mother, now exasperated, gave her a rude shove and obliged her to leave the room. Armando did not intercede. An eyebrow arched, and he appeared to be in deep reflection. At length he asked:

"*Señora,* did your sister buy the watch for herself?"

"No, *señor.* Our good friend Ismael, the one your friend spoke to you about, gave it to her for her birthday."

"I see." After some thought, he returned to his earlier question. "Please excuse my insistence, but what kept you so long at the market on the day of your sister's death?"

Lupe stirred uneasily in her chair. She regarded the lawyer helplessly. Miguel returned her glance with interest and urged·

"Try to remember."

"I've already told you," she replied. "I went out to get some medicine . . ." Suddenly her face brightened. "Now I remember! That was the day when two women got into a fight in the market-place, and I stood around watching the excitement. I even remember now that our friend Ismael arrived on the scene with the other officers and sent the women off in the police wagon. After-wards—yes—afterwards he bought some ice cream for my little girl . . ."

"Excellent!" exclaimed Armando. "That explains perfectly your delay. Now please, give me a bit more information about this Tomás, your sister's boyfriend."

"Well, he didn't seem like such a bad fellow. They'd been going together for quite some time, but several days ago they had a quarrel. I don't know what piece of gossip fell on Rosa's ears, but she was very burned up."

"Tomás customarily visited her here?" asked Armando.

"He used to come sometimes, but only when Juan wasn't here, because my husband didn't care much for the boy's informality towards the family."

"Did Tomás know that Rosa wouldn't be leaving the house on the day she died?"

"Let me see . . . yes. Yes, he knew. I remember that the day before when I was going shopping, I ran into him over in Nopal and told him that Rosa had a bad cold and that I wouldn't be letting her go out for several days."

"You had come across him by chance?"

"No. Tomás used to come and talk with me nearly every day with the hope that I'd be able to help him win over Rosa. Since he worked as a delivery boy, he was almost always around the streets. That day he told me that he had won on a lottery ticket and that he wanted to get married to Rosa . . . Just think of that!"

She began to cry. After a few moments, when she had calmed down somewhat, Armando asked her:

"Did Tomás know where your husband Juan worked?"

"Certainly. Tomás worked at the same place with him. That was how he met Rosa. It's a match factory, and one day when we all went to a party there, the young people met."

"Very well. Thank you very much, *señora*. I think for the time being we'll not have to bother you anymore."

The lawyer and his friend said goodbye and left. In the patio they found Rosita busily plucking feathers from a pigeon which she had tracked and caught. Armando gave her an affectionate pat and put a peso into her hand. The child promptly abandoned her captive and ran off in search of her mother.

Back at Zozaya's apartment, the two friends were discussing the matter.

"It would be advisable," Armando was saying, "to check and see if on the day in question there actually was a disturbance in the market of the sort that Lupe mentioned."

"It's already been checked and established," replied Miguel. "Juan called me to the police station immediately after they had arrested him and while I was there, I recall that Ismael Flores, the García's friend who is on the force, commented that on that day, the third of May it was, he had seen Lupe a *second* time after having chatted with her in the marketplace, when he received the call from the García's tenement."

"Who called the police?"

"One of the neighbors. As a matter of fact it was the woman in 10—*doña* Chona . . ."

The lawyer suddenly stopped speaking, as if a startling thought had struck him.

"What is it?" Zozaya asked.

"I just remembered what the other neighbor, Tula, told me."

"What's that?"

"She was at the market that day, too. And Lupe, she said, left the little girl with her while she went to the pharmacy . . ."

"Aha! So Lupe doesn't have an alibi after all!"

Zozaya burst out laughing when he saw the troubled expression on his friend's face. He said:

"Now you've really got yourself in a fix. In order to save the husband, you've got to implicate the wife. And the poor little daughter . . . Just imagine."

Miguel regarded him sorrowfully. "Do you actually think . . ."

"You're the one who's thinking it," replied Zozaya. "The wife suspects that her husband and her sister are deceiving her, jealousy blinds her, and she plans to dispose of her rival and, in the process, gain her revenge on the unfaithful husband. She goes to the market, leaves the child there with her neighbor, returns to the house, kills her sister with her husband's gun, takes the watch and hides it in Juan's clothing, and then hurries back to get her daughter. The family friend who invites them for ice cream is the ideal witness for establishing her alibi since, at the time the broken watch indicates, she is far away from the house in the company of a police officer."

"You're right," murmured Miguel, sadly, "it all checks."

"Everything, including the anonymous letter that she sends to her husband which arranges for him to go to a spot not too far from the house and leaves him looking mighty guilty."

"I never dreamed that Lupe might have been the murderer . . ."

"Well, not too fast, my friend. Notice that everything fits *except* the little detail that the watch that showed up in your client's pockets was not actually the dead girl's watch."

105

"You think, then, that the child is telling the truth?"

"Obviously."

"But isn't Lupe's attitude a strong argument against her? You saw how upset and confused she was when you asked her why she had delayed in the market that day, and how she became disturbed when the child claimed that the watch wasn't the right one."

"These arguments only have value when you can demonstrate a complete and convincing connection between them. Lupe's attitude in itself is not enough on which to base the assumption that she is the murderer. It could be that she actually was unable to recall the events of that morning; it could also very well be that she was nervous and impulsive owing to the difficult period she's going through. Attitude alone is not enough. You must prove that only the suspect, and no one else, could have committed the crime under each and all of the known circumstances."

"Well, then?"

"Consider this: the murderer has to be a person who knew the habits of the family, who knew that Juan worked at the match factory, who knew that Lupe went to the market, taking the little girl with her, every day at more or less the same time— a person who chose the day of Santa Cruz so that the shots wouldn't be noticed, and who knew, moreover, that that day Rosa would be home alone . . ."

"Then it's . . ."

"Wait a moment. The murderer, to be sure, planned the crime in advance. He sent an unsigned note to Juan and made an appointment for a place where there would probably not be witnesses who might testify on Juan's behalf. Notice that the contents of the letter reveal a man as its author, since a woman, even in self-defense, would scarcely accuse herself—though her mind might be plagued by jealousy and indignation—of being deceived. Besides, the message boy spoke of a 'gentleman.' So we have the murderer, as I was saying, arriving at the house shortly after Lupe had left. He was, without doubt, someone known to Rosa, since otherwise she wouldn't have opened the door to him. Then there was a struggle and during it the watch was shattered, probably by the gun when the girl raised her arm to protect herself. When the murderer saw the watch smashed beyond value, there was nothing he could do but hurry to a jewelry shop and buy another. He needed the watch, you realize, to establish the time of the murder. He bought another, carefully broke the crystal, and jammed the hands at the hour desired. Then he waited for the chance to slip it into Juan's clothing. Notice that Lupe, aside from not having the time to go out and buy a watch during the crucial period, didn't have the *money* to buy one."

"Of course. It all figures perfectly. Then it's Tomás who's the murderer. Really, he must have been seen entering the house."

"He might have been seen. He probably went between ten-thirty and eleven to see Rosa. Unquestionably, the crime had been committed by then, and . . ."

"What did you say?"

". . . he found the girl dead. He has said nothing about it for fear of being accused himself."

"But what do you mean. Haven't we determined the fact that Tomás is the murderer?"

"We haven't determined anything. You're the one who's suggesting it. Tell me something. Was Juan arrested at home or at the factory?"

"At the factory. The police went first to the scene of the crime at the tenement. Since the gun was Juan's, he was immediately a suspect, and they went to the factory for him. His absence from work during the morning naturally served to place suspicion on him and they arrested him."

Armando Zozaya said calmly, "Then the real murderer is Ismael Flores."

"The García's friend?"

"Precisely."

Miguel gazed in bewilderment at his friend. Armando explained with patience:

"Lupe could have had a motive, but she didn't have money to buy another watch and, what is most important, she couldn't have placed the new one in Juan's pocket, since Juan never came back home. Tomás fills almost all the requirements, and moreover he had the money necessary since he won on a lottery ticket, but he has no known motive and also had no opportunity of leaving the watch with Juan since he was not at the factory. Remember that as a delivery boy, his work was away from the factory. Flores, on the other hand, fits perfectly into the picture. He gave the watch to the girl which suggests he had more than a passing affection for her. Rosa had a boyfriend which would indicate that she had rejected Flores. And there we have the motive. But what irretrievably condemns him is the fact that he is the only person among the suspects who had the opportunity to transfer the watch into Juan's possession."

"When?"

"Obviously when he arrested him or when he took him to the police station. You know that it is customary to search all prisoners. This same Flores surreptitiously slipped the watch into one of the poor fellow's pockets and afterward ordered one of the other officers to finish the search of the prisoner. In this way, no one could ever suspect him. On the contrary, he was very kind, very good-hearted, he only wanted to help. Remember, too, that he kept Lupe in the marketplace with the entice- ment of the ice cream for the child so that Lupe would arrive home after the time indicated by the hands on the broken watch. The squabble between the women at the market was only a coin- cidence which happened to favor him, although it obliged him to hurry a great deal in his search for the new watch. The 'good friend of the family' was a sharp number, without a doubt."

"But how in the world am I going to prove his guilt?"

"Look for a jewelry shop where a man purchased two identi- cal watches within a relatively short time, and who, when he bought the second, brought along a broken one as an indication of what he wanted. The jeweler will doubtless remember. The child's declaration regarding the watch will be a fragile bit of evidence, but perhaps confronting Flores with the jeweler will produce something substantial. This is a classic case of circum- stantial evidence. It will all depend on your ability and luck in convincing the judge to withdraw the charge against Juan and reinstituting it against Flores."

Miguel left in a hurry for the Penitentiary. He scarcely mumbled a "*gracias, hermano*" before disappearing. Zozaya bade him farewell with a friendly wave of the hand. Then he lit a Raleigh, and contentedly smoothing his moustache, took up once again his reading of the short stories of Arkadio Averchenko.

FAR SOUTH
Dalmiro A. Sáenz

Dalmiro A. Sáenz has enjoyed wide popular acclaim in Argentina as the author of two collections of expertly told short narratives. He has also written several screenplays—some based on his own stories and novels—for Argentine films. As a playwright he has authored an avant-garde drama with the interesting title of Qwertyuiop. *Unusual titles are a Sáenz trademark. He has short-story collections entitled* Seventy Times Seven *and* Thirty-Thirty *as well as one called* No *in which one finds the title story as well as a story entitled "Yes." But his success is perhaps best explained by the unusual blending of a strict Catholic moral attitude with frequent scenes of considerable pornographic impact. "Far South," included in Sáenz's first book,* Seventy Times Seven *(1957), is one of his best tales. It is a laconic crime story set in the bleak southern expanse of Argentine Patagonia, where oil and sheep raising hold the only promises that lure men away from civilization to a wind-blown desolation.*

Far South

DALMIRO A. SÁENZ

I HEARD the story from a woman in Comodoro Rivadavia. It happened long ago, even before that unexpected outcome of the expectation of centuries which would attract men from faraway places to erect black towers against the limpid sky. Yes, it was before they found oil, long before. It happened during the time when the solitude of this country was rolled back by that white fleece which a three-year-old boy could find everywhere underfoot, and which, even though he could raise it over his head, was heavy enough to have permanently uprooted his parents from some distant place in Europe. Heavy enough, too, to push the pure, indefinite, and unjustifiable desert back against the foothills and the sea, with the continual bustle of the sociable animals whose weak and distant bleating was erased by the wind blowing through the gullies, whose distant and far-reaching tramplings traced out winding paths to their water holes and resting places.

The man lived some thirty leagues from Comodoro Rivadavia at a place called Pampa Fría. With him lived the woman whom he had met during one of his periodical trips to town, his two pack horses and countless dogs, and his elegant prancing chestnut mule which he rode with a saddle, having failed to accustom it to a halter.

He had met her there in the doorway of that house, on the street that would later be called San Martín, through which he would walk three or four times a year to buy his bag of fariña, or yerba maté and his provisions and a supply of liquor and tobacco and, later, flour and sugar, and, eventually, the woman herself who, after a brief exchange of glances and perhaps some

113

ceremonious touching of hands, would begin a type of idyll, memory, or simple affinity that would cause their neighbors to look up one morning to see the baggy form of the "Bulgarian" on his chestnut mule, surrounded by his dogs, with his pack horses laden with suitcases and saddlebags, and on top of it all, the woman—all heading east.

These two people lived there at Pampa Fría, constantly struggling against the grim elements, cooking the same meal and washing the same thick clothing, going out together on horseback to repair the sheep fold or chop firewood or clean the water, noticing the differences in their sexes only during the sheltered nights on top of the animal pelts stretched out on the kitchen floor, covered by the coarse frocks that both wore, in dull and primitive caresses which sometimes climaxed the tiring days, with the coals in the fire-pan still glowing, and the dogs outdoors alongside the horses' gear, growling at the night.

And then there were those mornings when the steaming maté, held between dirty fingers, and the twice-soldered silver *bombilla* were passed from one to the other during the long and silent hour during which they awaited the dawn, seated on the rough wooden benches which he finally abandoned to leave the kitchen in his peltskin gown, indifferent to the cold, feeling the crackling of the frost beneath his deformed sandals, carrying the shiny halter secured in his left arm, bearing himself the same way his father surely would have—and possibly even his grandfather—with the pail of milk or the heavy lantern on foggy mornings in his distant and vaguely remembered Bulgaria. And afterwards, he would return to the kitchen, now without the halter, to look for his *rebenque,* and go out again, while she, bent over a large tin, emptied the sediment from the maté gourd. Neither one perceived the least word or gesture that might denote a farewell, not a sign, nothing to indicate that separation of four, five, or six hours of two people united by that force which at times is greater than love or friendship, and amounting to identification, to reflection—a kind of comforting adjustment or a simple and desperate commonness of subsistence.

He would return after midday to ask:

"Put on the meat?"

"Yes."

Again the matés, one after another, in a serene silence interrupted by some random comment.

"Did Corbata let you handle him?"

"I had to put him up front, Toby got tired by hole."

"Yes, he's really a puppy. That cur's going to die on you some day."

"I know, I young too, I run, not die."

Again the silence, while the matés continued, and he would remove the grill from the oven and turn the meat.

"Are you going to work in the well today?"

"Yes. Work in the well."

The well excavation had been started years before in the infernally hard clay behind the house, in a stubborn, blind, single-minded attempt to locate water, beginning the day he saw some jonquil plants growing in that spot. It had provided nothing but months and months of pick-ax blows and unproductive wieldings of the shovel. Later on, with help from his wife and their bay mare, which he worked mercilessly at turning the pulley, his efforts brought him to a depth of twenty meters without revealing the least trace of water, or even moisture.

"You're going to have to have help if you're ever going to finish."

"*Don* Couyido to come next week to help us."

So it was. A week later, to the accompaniment of the dogs' furious growling, they saw Couyido, the Chilean, approaching, hardly visible in the windy distance, the forms of the man and his pack of hounds delineated against the sky.

He dismounted, with a series of coordinated movements of his large frame. He greeted the Bulgarian with a slow "*Buenas.*" Then he extended his hand to the woman, with his rigid arm and hard fingers and his gaze respectfully downcast beneath the greasy brim of his English cap.

They were days of hard work; the two men inside the well, and the woman with her bay mare, making never-ending turns with the pulley, and then emptying the bucket of golden clay.

115

There were a complex series of sparse movements and even fewer words than they could count on the fingers of one hand, and the accompaniment of dry sounds of earth and distance that indicated from the bottom of the well the rhythmic digging of the shovel and the sharp penetration of the pick, which would stop from time to time, while the squeak of the pulley's wheel denoted the gradual departure of the mare and the slow, upward journey of the bucket against the intense and lustrous blue circle which the edges of the pit carved out of the sky.

And upon completing the sluggish, laborious daily task, they tied the tools to the edge of the bucket that would then rise to the top where it was taken by the woman, who then lowered the rope on which first the Chilean, then the Bulgarian ascended, both grimy and sweaty. They washed themselves in the kitchen, while she unsaddled the bay mare and went into the house to await her turn at the tiled washbowl and the yellow towel.

She washed her hands and forearms and also her face, finishing the operation with a dunking of her stout head, tossing it back, and running her hands through her coarse hair in a decisive and masculine manner, her hardy features reflected in the piece of mirror that hung on a nail next to the empty soap dish alongside an old almanac with a smiling girl, which was suspended from the squalid and desolate kitchen wall.

And now the weighty and purposeless dialogue, a complement to the maté, with the almost unnecessary words used to express some idea nearly always related to animals, or to things, or already established facts, in an easy and comfortable exchange, followed by a silence filled with empty thoughts and opaque looks of weariness. Their faces, shining from their labors, caught in the static tension of their utterly simple lives, now began to loosen in relaxed contemplation of the flaming coals in the kitchen, or of the little games and movements of the black cat next to the small box beneath the table.

The three people lived there for many days, always together, eating, working, resting, and even sleeping side by side on the same floor of the sheltered kitchen, rising before dawn, separating only when the Bulgarian left to cut some brush or chop some

116

wood, thus leaving his wife with Couyido the Chilean in their silent and divided togetherness, the two at times exchanging a glance in a bold, daring, and almost curious manner across the unlimited barriers of their sexual distinction.

One time the two stood looking at each other across the table where she was preparing the dough for her cakes, amusing themselves with that crude, rudimentary, and initial flirtation that was repeated many times after, many days after, until one day, taking advantage of the temporary absence of the Bulgarian, he embraced her against the kitchen wall, in a pure and understandable show of emotion to which she responded by slapping him lightly, in a kind of delicate caress, of almost curious acknowledgement, and then they kissed brusquely and pulled apart and kissed again, with the crude vehemence of their awkward and innocent novelty.

"Do you want to come with me?"

"Where to?"

"I've got a thousand pesos in the drawer; I won it at cards."

"What about the Bulgarian?"

"Leave him to me."

"What are you going to do?"

"I already have it worked out. Tomorrow after twelve when we finish working, we'll tie the tools to the bucket, and you haul it up. Then you lower the rope and I'll go up first as usual. After that we don't lower the rope any more and we leave. Nobody comes by here. He'll be all alone there in the bottom, and if someone finds him, it'll look like an accident."

"No, I can't do that. He's a very good man."

"You want to spend all your life with that Bulgarian?"

"No."

"All right, then, we have to do something."

"Yes, we have to do something."

The Bulgarian arrived later with the heap of wood he had chopped and threw it in a box saying:

"*Don* Couyido, you sleep now and early tomorrow you can do skinning."

"All right."

117

"By low hill you find traps. Watch for dogs; I put out poison."

"A lot of foxes this year?"

"Yes, enough."

"How many pelts do you have now?"

"Nineteen."

"That's good."

And the following morning, before dawn, Couyido left, the collar of his poncho turned up, after pausing momentarily in the doorway of the kitchen. When the crackling of his steps on the frost was lost in the darkness of the dawn, the Bulgarian reached over quickly and shook his wife.

"Wake up, wake up."

"What? What's the matter?"

"He have thousand pesos in drawer."

"Who? What's the matter with you? What are you saying?"

"*Don* Couyido have thousand pesos in drawer."

"So what?"

"Later we leave him in well. First you send up tools; then I come up first and he stay down. We keep thousand pesos."

"What do you mean?"

"With thousand pesos we can find land on other side with good water so we not have to stay here rest of our life. We have to do something."

"Yes, we have to do something."

That afternoon the three members of the double conspiracy resumed their work, the outcome of which was to depend on the woman whose abrupt and firm steps beside the bay mare mixed impressions of sandals with hoofprints. Meanwhile, the men down below bent silently over their work. Both labored, not in the search of distant water, but in the addition of a few centimeters to that tomb where each would die of hunger and thirst, without hate or desperation, without lust or greed, but obeying the simple principle of taking whatever one needed and respecting the overpowering logic imposed by the desert—an act whose consequences, viewed, softened, and almost forgiven now at a distant point in time and space, make us understand the force that allowed Argentina to colonize, spread out, and finally civilize that immense land called Patagonia.

And then the moment came to finish working. They filled the pail with golden clay for the last time, tied the shovel and pick to the rope which rose slowly up to the black pulley, and rested there calmly next to the sky. The men looked up and waited and waited. Then came the steps of the bay mare. And then the silence of the lonely earth.

Translated from the Spanish by Michael G. Gafner

A SCRAP OF TINFOIL
Alfonso Ferrari Amores

Alfonso Ferrari Amores is a porteño (*native of Buenos Aires*) *by birth and it is in the Argentine capital that he has established his reputation as a highly competent and versatile journalist, author, and playwright. For nearly half a century he has contributed articles and features to Buenos Aires newspapers and magazines. As an author he has probably written (under several English-sounding pseudonyms) more detective novels than any other Spanish American writer, and he may well hold the record for detective stories in Spanish also. Add to this his credentials as a prize-winning dramatist and radio script writer and his past successes as a composer of tangos and you have an impression of the varied career of Alfonso Ferrari Amores. His short stories of crime and detection have not been collected and there are many fine stories lying forgotten in back issues of such fondly remembered but now deceased Argentine magazines as* Leoplán *and* Vea y Lea. *One of these stories is "A Scrap of Tinfoil," an ingenious tale of murder, a brilliant "perfect crime" idea laid in the same harsh Patagonian setting as the preceding story by Dalmiro A. Sáenz. It is fortunate that this very short short story has been saved from oblivion. It may be Ferrari's best.*

A Scrap of Tinfoil

ALFONSO FERRARI AMORES

JOACO MIGUELES, my wine-loving friend and philosopher, winked at me as he gulped a mouthful of Mendozan *tinto*.

"Look here," he said. He set down his glass and took from his pocket a neatly folded sheet of tinfoil, the kind that comes with chocolate bars and cigarettes.

"Waterproofing for the roof," he said, smiling proudly. "I found it on the road today. It's perfect for the job."

I looked up between the rafters of the little shack Joaco shared with his second wife, far out on the Argentine sand dunes of La Magdalena. The glistening blue sky of the hot afternoon was cutting through in a few places with scorching shafts that appeared to be burning the holes bigger as I watched.

"No time to waste, friend," I said, clouding his contented grin. "I heard thunder on my way over. We'll have rain soon, and I'd better be leaving."

"Oh, no, no, no!" he exclaimed. "Stay and talk a little more. It's a lonely existence out here on this desert. And when the wife is out—" He gazed sadly at me, patting his wine glass as if it, too, were a dear friend. (Joaco's wine glasses were more the size of vases, since he could splash in virtually the entire contents of a bottle of wine in one pouring.)

"Well," I said hesitatingly, "perhaps one half-hour more."

He sighed happily and leaned back noisily in his wicker chair across the table from me.

One thing about my companion which made him tolerable company on these unbearably hot days was his unpolished but certain gift for conversation. Or, perhaps better put, for solilo-

123

quy. So I knew the reason he wanted me to linger before returning to the city was not that he wished to hear my voice. On the
contrary—

"This scrap of tinfoil here, my friend," he began, indicating
the sheet of wrapping he had smoothed out carefully on the
table. "It carries a very worthwhile lesson." Joaco looked at me
from under his bleached and bushy eyebrows to see if I were
interested. I nodded noncommittally.

"It shows one that no matter how poor a man's existence"—
with a gesture he indicated his humble dwelling—"he can better
it by taking advantage of any small windfall that may come his
way."

"Yes, I suppose you're right," I commented, reaching over to
fill my glass and irrigate my throat, which had become parched
from the hot dry air of the region.

Joaco sat in silence for a moment, tugging pensively at his
lower lip. Presently, he cleared his throat and said: "It reminds
me of something, you know. I once lived in Patagonia—years
ago, when I was young. It was a miserable life there, but it
taught me to be satisfied with what I have now."

"Well, that's nice," I said.

"I was poor as a beggar then. It was in Río Negro—El
Ñireco, to be exact. For many months I lived in an old cement
water tank which I had converted to a sleeping room. All the
other fellows were making decent money working on the road
gangs. But not me.

"I wasn't cut out to work from sun-up to sunset like a pack
horse. So I just kept on as poor as ever. What I've told you of
my modest living quarters will suffice to explain why, when the
snows began, I didn't find it hard to choose between my little
water tank and a cot in the back room of an herb grower's shop
in Viedma, where they offered me a job as clerk. With a choice
like that, who's going to hesitate?

"So there I was—the sole occupant of the shop—when one
day who should stroll in but wealthy *don* Hellmuth, the most

124

infamous miser and wife-beater in the province. A shady, under-handed character, too, if ever there was one! Well, this day we chatted about a thousand things—this and that—and ultimately came around to the subject of herbs.

"At an appropriate moment I mentioned casually to him my theory that if it were true that diabetes consisted of an excess of glucose in the blood stream, it seemed to me that the eating of poisonous mushrooms, which kill by depriving the blood of the same substance, could be effective—in determined doses—in curing diabetics. It was a simple question of logic.

"*Don* Hellmuth thought a moment, then asked me: 'Do you have any poisonous mushrooms here?'

"My only answer was to reach down and take two sacks from behind the counter and lay them before him.

" 'These are the good ones,' I said, smiling, 'The others are poisonous. They look a lot alike, don't they?'

"*Don* Hellmuth agreed, marvelling at the identical appearance of the varieties.

" 'Just imagine,' I continued. 'If they were served separately on two plates, no one could distinguish the poisonous ones from the others. Of course, it would be handy to have the antidote ready—just in case.'

" 'What would that be?' *don* Hellmuth asked, revealing great interest in this matter of poisonous mushrooms. I had judged him shrewdly.

" 'The same glucose we were speaking of. A very concen-trated solution. It could be swallowed or injected.' "

" 'Give me some of both kinds of mushrooms,' he said impet-uously. 'And the antidote!'

"As I was collecting for the mushrooms and the bottle of antidote, I said: 'Of course, if the antidote were within reach of —um—an enemy who might have eaten the poisonous mush-rooms, it would be wise to disguise it, so that he would not find and take it.'

" 'How's that?' *don* Hellmuth asked, looking at me narrowly.

"I opened a drawer and took out a label with a red skull and

125

crossbones on it, and below, the word POISON. I glued it to the antidote bottle.

" 'There,' I said. 'Now only you and I know that this is not what the label says. Try not to forget this point, my friend!'

"By chance, that very night *don* Hellmuth's wife came to take refuge in my shop. She was young and very beautiful, a native girl whom *don* Hellmuth—the gringo!—used to beat unmercifully.

"She told me how, after supping on a mushroom stew, he had thrown her out of the house, chasing her with a whip. *Don* Hellmuth, as mean as he was rich and tightfisted, fell into such fits of anger frequently, but it seems that he had never had one like this before. Ah me! The girl was crying like a baby! And women were so scarce in those parts.

"So I rang up on the telephone, asked for *don* Hellmuth's line and, the moment I heard his voice, cried out excitedly. 'Listen! I made a mistake with the mushroom labels. Hurry! The harmless ones are poisonous, and the . . .'

"I heard that they found him the next day—dead from a dose of cyanide. The doctor analyzed the contents of the bottle that *don* Hellmuth had drained completely, and said:

" 'Poison. Just as the label says. Obviously, *don* Hellmuth committed suicide.'

"Afterward, of course, there were those who looked at me suspiciously because I married his widow. Ah, she was a prize, to be sure!"

The sky had darkened now, and the sound of thunder came again, resounding over the limitless stretch of arid plains. Joaco glanced up at the holes in the roof of the hut, then turned his gaze down on the piece of tinfoil on the table. He smiled.

"She was my scrap of tinfoil. Just like this bit I found today —something to help improve my humble existence." He chuckled softly. "Humph. You can imagine what a cause for gossip our marriage was. A source of endless chatter among the envious fellows, that's all. Bah, they see the mark of money on everything. Why couldn't they understand that a man, no matter how poor he might be, could still be disinterested?"

I shook my head slowly and rose to leave. But Joaco placed a hand on my sleeve.

"They did the routine autopsy on *don* Hellmuth soon afterward. And that was how they proved, incidentally, that the mushrooms he ate were harmless."

Joaco winked at me again, lifted his glass before his eyes, and gazed at it appreciatively, a little absently. "What did they think anyway? That *I'd* be selling poisonous mushrooms!"

THE CASE OF THE "SOUTHERN ARROW"
L. A. Isla

The previous two stories have as their setting the south of Argentina—Patagonia. L. A. Isla's "The Case of the 'Southern Arrow' " deals in part with an area situated directly west across the Andes Mountains in the south of Chile. This selection is taken from Isla's short-story collection entitled Murder in Forestal Park *(1946), on the cover of which the publishers insinuate that the author's name is a pseudonym and that there is reason to believe that "Isla" has actually lived the experiences he attributes to his detective character, Inspector De la Barra of the Santiago, Chile, police force. There is, indeed, a convincing air about the present story that recounts a murder aboard a crack train running from the south of Chile to the capital. The clues seem plausible, the investigation follows a reasonable course, and the solution is reached in a perfectly natural fashion. Fact or fiction, "The Case of the 'Southern Arrow' " is an attractive example of the relatively infrequent Chilean detective short story that rejects exotic foreign settings and lays its scene in a specific Chilean locale.*

The Case of the "Southern Arrow"

L. A. ISLA

THE case in question here, which occurred nearly two years ago, was one of the few that Inspector De la Barra took part in when I was not at his side. The inspector is not, generally speaking, in favor of his exploits receiving public attention. But on one occasion, when I had been invited to his house for dinner with Alvear and another fellow who worked with us, we were treated to his account of the case of the "Southern Arrow."

I don't recall exactly what we were talking about as we were enjoying an after-dinner coffee, but the conversation eventually came around to the subject of journeys through the extraordinarily beautiful southern regions of Chile.

"I can't see how a person can help but be embarrassed to admit he doesn't know the south," said Alvear. "Many people think that Santiago is Chile and haven't the slightest qualm about admitting that they have no idea of what lies beyond Valparaiso or Rancagon."

(Alvear was proud of having been born in a small town in the south and he never let an occasion pass without making this fact quite clear.)

"Most assuredly," replied De la Barra, "we have breathtaking things in Chile. Nonetheless, nowadays more and more Chileans are demonstrating an interest in the southern part of the country. Only a few years ago, eighty-nine percent of the tourists who visited the southern lake region were either Argentines or Yankees."

"People feel more like travelling today," I said, "and mainly, I think, because of the improved tourist facilities that are avail-

131

able now. Train travel, for example. You know, the 'Southern Arrow' can get you from Santiago to Osorno in just a few hours."

"By the way, Inspector," said Alvear, "have you ever travelled on the 'Southern Arrow'?"

"Two or three times," replied De la Barra. "I have some very interesting recollections of a case that occurred during my first trip on that express. I don't know if you've ever heard about it."

We urged him to tell us the story.

"I don't recall exactly when the 'Arrow' began to run," he said. "It must have been in mid- or late December of 1940. Early in January of 1940 I had to travel Concepción to draw up an indictment. I'd been working on the job for around four days when I received a telegram from the Commission, ordering me to return to the capital as soon as possible. I handed over the indictment and decided to take the 'Arrow' on the trip back. It came through San Rosendo at about eleven-fifteen in the morning after having pulled out of Temuco at seven.

"Some fifteen or twenty people go on with me at San Rosendo, among whom I discovered an old friend, a ranch owner by the name of Hurtado, who was going to Santiago to close a business deal. He and I, together with a railroad detective named Escobar who had left with the train from Temuco, made up a congenial group.

"A little after one, we went to the dining car for lunch. While we were eating, Hurtado pointed out a middle-aged man, gray-haired and quite well-dressed, who was sipping a cold drink with a straw.

" 'Do you know that fellow?' Hurtado asked me. 'That's *don* Mariano del Campo. He's wealthy enough to buy the "Arrow" with the small change he's carrying in his billfold. Unfortunately, his marriage is in bad shape. His wife lives in Concepción. She's quite a bit younger. The other chap with him, the one drinking beer, is his assistant—a private secretary of sorts.'

"The person Hurtado was referring to was a slender young man, elegantly dressed in black. He wore glasses and had a large Adam's apple that bobbed up and down as he drank his beer.

We returned to our seats and, a few minutes later, saw *señor* Del Campo and his aide pass by. Their seats were further back on the train.

"We spent the afternoon chatting and thumbing through magazines. There must have been at least sixty people on the train and many of them, especially the women, had tilted their seats back and were dozing, no doubt because of the oppressive heat.

"We were soon approaching Santiago; the 'Arrow' was scheduled to arrive around four or four-fifteen. Escobar invited me to have a stroll through the train, so we left Hurtado behind, sleeping peacefully. In one of the cars to the rear I passed Del Campo, who was evidently also asleep, slumped against the window with his chin on his chest. His hat was covering his face. His secretary was nowhere to be seen, and I imagined he had gone to the club car. It turned out I was right, for when Escobar and I went to have a drink, there he was, wobbling his Adam's apple as he downed a glass of fruit juice.

"We were still in the club car when the train pulled into Santiago. I said goodbye to Escobar, who had to report to his office at the train station, and got off the train with Hurtado.

" 'I haven't been to Santiago in ages,' my friend said, as we headed out of the station. 'I don't imagine it's changed much since the last time. It must have been in '33 or '34 . . .'

"Over the uproar of travellers and porters I suddenly heard my name being called. Escobar came running towards us.

" '*Señor* De la Barra!' he said, panting and taking my arm. 'Please . . . come with me . . . You were on the train . . . Someone's been strangled! It's the man who was travelling with his secretary.'

" '*Don* Mariano del Campo!' exclaimed Hurtado, turning pale. 'It can't be! You must be joking!'

"We hurried back to the platform. A crowd of onlookers had already formed beside the 'Southern Arrow.'

" 'Has everyone who was on the train gotten off already?' I asked Escobar.

" 'There are five or six persons who hadn't gotten off yet

133

when the secretary discovered the body. It'll be impossible to locate the others.'

"We got back on the train. There, in his seat, in the same position in which we'd seen him the first time, was *señor* Del Campo. His hat had been removed and we could see now that the collar of his white shirt was bloodstained. There was a group of passengers standing in the aisle: a woman who was pushing forward trying to get a better view, two or three railroad employees, and the dead man's secretary. The latter looked terribly shaken and was wringing his hands.

"Bending over the body, I could make out a thin red line across the victim's throat, like that left on the skin when a wire or a cord is tightened across it. Just then a bespectacled man dressed in a blue suit addressed me.

" 'Are you with the police?' he asked.

"I said I was.

" 'I'm a doctor,' he said, offering me his card. 'I've been on the train since Temuco. Would you like me to have a look at him?'

"I agreed, but cautioned him not to disturb the position of the victim. He took out a handkerchief and, wrapping it around his hand, lifted the victim's head by tilting his forehead back. We could then see clearly that the red line across the throat was really a deep wound, especially beneath the chin, from which, however, he had not bled profusely.

"We heard a muffled cry. It was the woman who had been trying to look over the head of the others. She must have seen too much because she had to be helped to a seat, nearly in a faint.

" 'Death by asphyxia,' said the doctor. 'The trachea is completely flattened, although it is not shattered. To judge from the appearance of the wound, it was inflicted by a piano wire or some such fine cord. All it took was a good pull and then hanging on for a few moments. A very effective and seldom used technique.' (The autopsy that was later performed confirmed the doctor's observations.)

134

"Of the passengers on the 'Arrow,' aside from the four who hadn't managed to get off and Del Campo's secretary, we were able to locate only six who, owing to delays in claiming their baggage, remained in the station and were apprehended before they reached the street. But they had either been seated in other cars or had seats in front of Del Campo and didn't see a thing. In short, nobody knew anything.

"Del Campo's secretary, whose name was Carlos Alfaro, was questioned at length and stuck very convincingly to his story. After having lunch in the diner, he and Del Campo went back to their seats. Alfaro read for half an hour, then fell asleep. When he woke up, the train was approaching Santiago and he saw that Del Campo was apparently still sleeping. Not wanting to wake him, he went alone to the club car. That part we could attest to, for that was when we saw him there. The question is: was Del Campo already dead when Alfaro thought he was sleeping? The medical report indicated that Del Campo had died thirty minutes or less before the train reached Santiago. When the train was passing through Alameda, Alfaro went back to his seat and started getting the baggage together. He thought it strange that Del Campo was still sleeping. Finally, when nearly all the other passengers had left the train he tried to waken him. He realized immediately that his employer was dead.

"One interesting fact emerges from Alfaro's account: so far as we know, there was no one on the train who was an acquaintance of the victim. Who, then, had committed the crime, and why? Del Campo was carrying a sizable amount of money in cash on his person. It hadn't been touched. Clearly, then, there was some kind of revenge involved.

"Do you see how fascinating it is that the crime was committed during a train trip? The murderer ran the constant risk of being discovered while in the act of committing the crime. Anyone could have seen him. We must assume he waited until most of the passengers were reading or sleeping and, of course, the secretary was gone to the club car. We determined later that all the seats in front and to the rear of Del Campo had been

135

vacant, except, of course, for the one immediately behind him. The murderer had occupied that one. From all appearances, we had to assume, therefore, that the crime was committed to prevent Del Campo from reaching Santiago alive.

"Alfaro stated that his employer had gone to Concepción to have a discussion with his wife, who lived there in the home of some friends, and from whom he had been separated for quite some time. The purpose of the talk was to reach an agreement by which the marriage could be annulled. The secretary had no knowledge of the results of their meeting, for Del Campo always maintained a certain reserve with respect to his marital affairs.

"When we asked if anyone recalled seeing the person who was seated behind Del Campo, we got a wide assortment of replies. Someone recalled a tall man, two other people a girl dressed in black. Five people thought the seat had been vacant. The rest had no idea at all.

"As for myself, I wasn't sure. When I walked by with Escobar, I paid most attention, of course to Del Campo—because of what Hurtado had told me about him. Nevertheless, I had the impression that the occupant of the seat immediately to the rear was a man and that he was reading a magazine when we passed by.

"At my request I was put in charge of the case and received authorization the next day to return to Concepción. I was convinced that the key to the solution of the crime was to be found in the person of Del Campo's wife. She had lived with friends in Concepción for more than a year. She received me in the drawing room of a very elegant residence. She, too, was elegant. (In fact, I got the feeling that her friends were living with her in *her* house.) She was ravishing—about thirty, blonde, and with a rather superior air about her.

"Before I told her who I was, she asked me if I were a friend of her husband. I said I was.

" 'Did you know Mariano for long?'

" 'About two years.'

" 'This has been a terrible blow for me,' she said. 'Imagine seeing him leave in the morning, alive and well, and then receiving a telegram that same day telling me what had happened! I have hesitated to return to Santiago—because of his family. His brothers . . . are not fond of me. Perhaps you knew that.'

" 'Vaguely, yes,' I replied. 'Your husband was planning to annul the marriage, isn't that so?'

" 'He came here to ask for that. But I refused. All of our problems have been caused by gossip. You know how people can talk. In our case, it was the members of his family.'

" 'But he was prepared to terminate the marriage,' I said.

" 'Yes, that's true. Mariano was very weak. Weak in his character. He believed everything his brothers said. They finally made our life intolerable and I decided to come to Concepción. I have relatives here.'

" '*Señora,*' I said. 'Are you aware that your husband was— murdered?'

" 'The telegrams I have received inferred that. It's unbelievable. Was it robbery?'

" 'No. It is apparent that robbery was not the motive.'

" 'How strange! Mariano had no enemies, at least that I'm aware of. But what other explanation can there be?'

"She gave the impression of being very upset, but in a controlled way, choosing her words carefully. Of course, you had to keep in mind the fact that she had been separated from her husband for more than a year. I talked with her for at least half an hour, but without discovering anything that seemed of value to the investigation. However, as I was leaving the house I remembered something she had said: 'All of our problems have been caused by gossip.'

"What kind of gossip? What, I wondered, were the specific details? I have quite a few friends in Concepción, aside from my professional colleagues. In the neighborhood where Del Campo's widow lived I knew two married couples. The wives turned out to be most helpful and three hours later I was in possession of a number of highly interesting bits of information.

"According to the neighborhood grapevine, *señora* Del Campo was deceiving her husband with a man who worked at the Asturias Club, a fashionable cabaret located in Concepción. The establishment had opened only recently and the friend of

137

Del Campo's wife was apparently a combination of part-time owner and band musician. No one, however, was able to produce the fellow's name.

"I fell back on the reliable service of the Concepción police. At Headquarters I found out what I wanted from a young police officer named Cáceres who knew the city like the palm of his hand.

" 'The man you're referring to,' he told me, 'is an Italian by the name of Zanelli. He plays the violin or something of the sort.'

"A connection between the murderer and Zanelli leapt instantly into my mind. Instead of wire or a thin cord, Del Campo could have been strangled with a violin string. That night I went with Cáceres to the Asturias Club. We arrived there around nine o'clock.

" 'Is Zanelli here at this time?' I asked Cáceres.

" ' I don't know,' he replied. 'I come by here only when I'm on night duty, so it's usually later than this. Sometimes I see him, sometimes I don't.'

" 'By any chance do you remember seeing Zanelli two nights ago?'

" 'I'm not sure,' he replied, gazing across the dance floor to where the orchestra was playing. 'Zanelli's not on now,' he said. 'Since he's apparently some kind of manager, too, he doesn't play all the time. He may show up later or, I suppose, he could be in the office now.'

"We sat down and waited. The place was filling up rapidly. The cigarette smoke grew denser by the moment and the stuffiness became uncomfortable. We had been there for some twenty minutes when Cáceres said quietly, 'There he is, Inspector. By the piano.'

"I looked through the smoky haze and saw an elegantly dressed man leaning against a column at the far end of the dance floor. Dressed in a tuxedo and smoking a cigarette, he was idly observing the dancers. I wondered if I was looking at a murderer. For an instant I was sure I was mistaken. Then it

138

occurred to me that I might as well continue pretending it was all an error. I called a waiter.

" 'Would you please ask *señor* Zanelli if he would care to join us for a few moments?'

"When Zanelli received the message, he looked across at us sharply. There was a moment of indecision, then he headed in our direction, making his way around the dance floor with long, firm strides.

"I got up and shook his hand. 'I never expected I'd run into you here,' I said. 'I thought you'd be in Santiago. It's a coincidence that we've both returned to Concepción.'

" 'I'm afraid you're mistaken, *señor*,' he replied. 'I think we are meeting now for the first time.'

" 'But no, *señor* Zanelli. You *are* Zanelli, aren't you?'

" 'Yes, but—'

" 'I guess you don't remember. We met Wednesday on the "Southern Arrow." '

"I could see that he was shaken. He wrinkled his brow. 'Just who are you, please? This really is the first time—'

" 'Come now. You're joking, of course. Here, my friend, sit down and have a drink with us.'

"By then he must have concluded that I was drunk, because he forced an unsuccessful smile and shrugged. I offered him my untouched drink and he took it hesitatingly. It was then that I saw his right hand. Along the side I noted three or four straight, parallel cuts in his flesh. They were visible only because the creases stood out clearly against the whiteness of his skin.

"When we arrested him, we found that on his left hand he had a set of matching marks. He was unable to give any sensible explanation of how he had come by them. When I suggested they might have been inflicted by a violin string, he refused to say anything.

"We brought him face-to-face with *señora* Del Campo. After a rather theatrical scene, Zanelli confessed that he had killed her husband because, as he put it, he had 'some accounts to settle with him.' He would not say anything more to clarify that state-

139

ment. I rather think that the 'accounts' were not with the victim, because Zanelli turned out to be up to his neck in debts of all kinds.

"Through the entire affair, Zanelli maintained the haughtiness of an operatic tenor—a posture very faithful to his Italian heritage. From the widow's statements we determined that Zanelli was an incurable big-scale spender. Apparently she had indicated to him that if she were ever to be widowed, she would agree to marry him. Zanelli built a glorious future on that idea. When he learned that Del Campo was determined to ask for an annulment—after which the wife would receive only alimony payments (an insignificant income, to Zanelli's way of thinking) —he decided to carry out the crime. Too refined to use a revolver or some other instrument of violence, he dreamed up the idea of strangling his victim with the violin string. In his home we found the violin from which it had been taken. The string itself, Zanelli told us, he had tossed into the Bio-Bio River on his way back to Concepción."

"What an egotistical plan!" exclaimed Alvear, greatly impressed by De la Barra's account. "What happened to the widow, Inspector?"

"She was able to show that she was innocent of any complicity in the crime," De la Barra replied. "All she had done was inform Zanelli that her husband was making the trip to Santiago on the 'Southern Arrow.' When the excitement subsided, I think she went to live in Bueños Aires. Zanelli was sentenced to twenty years."

"Imagine that character twiddling his thumbs for all that time," commented Alvear. "And they probably never let him play his violin."

JUST LATHER, THAT'S ALL
Hernando Téllez

The late Colombian essayist and short-story writer Hernando Téllez was not a prolific writer. His reputation as an author of prose fiction is based mainly on the stories of Ashes for the Wind and Other Tales, *which he published in Bogotá in 1950. Among the stories included in that volume is one which has carried Téllez's name far beyond the borders of his native land. "Just Lather, That's All" has been widely anthologized both in Spanish America, in the U.S., and abroad. It is read in Spanish in this country in college-level reading texts and in English in paperback anthologies. In 1972 the* Reader's Digest *will include it in a new collection of "best" stories from all over the world. What is the appeal of this succinct little story? There are murders in it (so numerous the number is not certain), yet it is not about crime. Nothing really happens in it (a man gets shaved), yet it is a tense and compelling narrative. It seems to deal with a barber but at the end the reader is surprised into realizing that it really does not. And beneath it all is a stark demonstration of Latin "machismo," or exaggerated courage and manliness. It has its human side, too. Quite honestly, it merits a place in anyone's anthology.*

Just Lather, That's All
HERNANDO TÉLLEZ

HE said nothing when he entered. I was passing the best of my razors back and forth on a strop. When I recognized him I started to tremble. But he didn't notice. Hoping to conceal my emotion, I continued sharpening the razor. I tested it on the meat of my thumb, and then held it up to the light.

At that moment he took off the bullet-studded belt that his gun holster dangled from. He hung it up on a wall hook and placed his military cap over it. Then he turned to me, loosening the knot of his tie, and said, "It's hot as hell. Give me a shave." He sat in the chair.

I estimated he had a four-day beard—the four days taken up by the latest expedition in search of our troops. His face seemed reddened, burned by the sun. Carefully, I began to prepare the soap. I cut off a few slices, dropped them into the cup, mixed in a bit of warm water, and began to stir with the brush. Immediately the foam began to rise. "The other boys in the group should have this much beard, too," he remarked. I continued stirring the lather.

"But we did all right, you know. We got the main ones. We brought back some dead, and we got some others still alive. But pretty soon they'll all be dead."

"How many did you catch?" I asked.

"Fourteen. We had to go pretty deep into the woods to find them. But we'll get even. Not one of them comes out of this alive, not one."

He leaned back on the chair when he saw me with the lather-covered brush in my hand. I still had to put the sheet on him. No doubt about it, I was upset. I took a sheet out of a drawer

143

and knotted it around his neck. He wouldn't stop talking. He probably thought I was in sympathy with his party.

"The town must have learned a lesson from what we did," he said.

"Yes," I replied, securing the knot at the base of his dark, sweaty neck.

"That was a fine show, eh?"

"Very good," I answered, turning back for the brush.

The man closed his eyes with a gesture of fatigue and sat waiting for the cool caress of the soap. I had never had him so close to me. The day he ordered the whole town to file into the patio of the school to see the four rebels hanging there, I came face to face with him for an instant. But the sight of the mutilated bodies kept me from noticing the face of the man who had directed it all, the face I was now about to take into my hands.

It was not an unpleasant face, and the beard, which made him look a bit older than he was, didn't suit him badly at all. His name was Torres—Captain Torres. A man of imagination, because who else would have thought of hanging the naked rebels and then holding target practice on their bodies?

I began to apply the first layer of soap. With his eyes closed, he continued. "Without any effort I could go straight to sleep," he said, "but there's plenty to do this afternoon."

I stopped the lathering and asked with a feigned lack of interest, "A firing squad?"

"Something like that, but a little slower."

I got on with the job of lathering his beard. My hands started trembling again. The man could not possibly realize it, and this was in my favor. But I would have preferred that he hadn't come. It was likely that many of our faction had seen him enter. And an enemy under one's roof imposes certain conditions.

I would be obliged to shave that beard like any other one, carefully, gently, like that of any customer, taking pains to see that no single pore emitted a drop of blood. Being careful to see that the little tufts of hair did not lead the blade astray. Seeing that his skin ended up clean, soft, and healthy, so that passing

144

the back of my hand over it I couldn't feel a hair. Yes, I was secretly a rebel, but I was also a conscientious barber, and proud of the precision required of my profession.

I took the razor, opened up the two protective arms, exposed the blade, and began the job—from one of the sideburns downward. The razor responded beautifully. His beard was inflexible and hard, not too long, but thick. Bit by bit the skin emerged. The razor rasped along, making its customary sound as fluffs of lather, mixed with bits of hair, gathered along the blade.

I paused a moment to clean it, then took up the strop again to sharpen the razor, because I'm a barber who does things properly. The man, who had kept his eyes closed, opened them now, removed one of his hands from under the sheet, felt the spot on his face where the soap had been cleared off, and said, "Come to the school today at six o'clock."

"The same thing as the other day?" I asked, horrified.

"It could be even better," he said.

"What do you plan to do?"

"I don't know yet. But we'll amuse ourselves." Once more he leaned back and closed his eyes. I approached with the razor poised.

"Do you plan to punish them all?" I ventured timidly.

"All."

The soap was drying on his face. I had to hurry. In the mirror I looked towards the street. It was the same as ever—the grocery store with two or three customers in it. Then I glanced at the clock—2:20 in the afternoon.

The razor continued on its downward stroke. Now from the other sideburn down. A thick, blue beard. He should have let it grow like some poets or priests do. It would suit him well. A lot of people wouldn't recognize him. Much to his benefit, I thought, as I attempted to cover the neck area smoothly.

There, surely, the razor had to be handled masterfully, since the hair, although softer, grew into little swirls. A curly beard. One of the tiny pores could open up and issue forth its pearl of blood, but a good barber prides himself on never allowing this to happen to a customer.

145

How many of us had he ordered shot? How many of us had he ordered mutilated? It was better not to think about it. Torres did not know that I was his enemy. He did not know it nor did the rest. It was a secret shared by very few, precisely so that I could inform the revolutionaries of what Torres was doing in the town and of what he was planning each time he undertook a rebel-hunting excursion.

So it was going to be very difficult to explain that I had him right in my hands and let him go peacefully—alive and shaved.

The beard was now almost completely gone. He seemed younger, less burdened by years than when he had arrived. I suppose this always happens with men who visit barber shops. Under the stroke of my razor Torres was being rejuvenated— rejuvenated because I am a good barber, the best in the town, if I may say so.

How hot it is getting! Torres must be sweating as much as I. But he is a calm man, who is not even thinking about what he is going to do with the prisoners this afternoon. On the other hand I, with this razor in my hands—I stroking and restroking this skin, can't even think clearly.

Damn him for coming! I'm a revolutionary, not a murderer. And how easy it would be to kill him. And he deserves it. Does he? No! What the devil! No one deserves to have someone else make the sacrifice of becoming a murderer. What do you gain by it? Nothing. Others come along and still others, and the first ones kill the second ones, and they the next ones—and it goes on like this until everything is a sea of blood.

I could cut this throat just so—*zip, zip!* I wouldn't give him time to resist and since he has his eyes closed he wouldn't see the glistening blade or my glistening eyes. But I'm trembling like a real murderer. Out of his neck a gush of blood would spout onto the sheet, on the chair, on my hands, on the floor. I would have to close the door. And the blood would keep inching along the floor, warm, ineradicable, uncontainable, until it reached the street, like a little scarlet stream.

I'm sure that one solid stroke, one deep incision, would prevent any pain. He wouldn't suffer. But what would I do with

146

the body? Where would I hide it? I would have to flee, leaving all I have behind, and take refuge far away. But they would follow until they found me. "Captain Torres' murderer. He slit his throat while he was shaving him—a coward."

And then on the other side. "The avenger of us all. A name to remember. He was the town barber. No one knew he was defending our cause."

Murderer or hero? My destiny depends on the edge of this blade. I can turn my hand a bit more, press a little harder on the razor, and sink it in. The skin would give way like silk, like rubber. There is nothing more tender than human skin and the blood is always there, ready to pour forth.

But I don't want to be a murderer. You came to me for a shave. And I perform my work honorably . . . I don't want blood on my hands. Just lather, that's all. You are an executioner and I am only a barber. Each person has his own place in the scheme of things.

Now his chin had been stroked clean and smooth. The man sat up and looked into the mirror. He rubbed his hands over his skin and felt it fresh, like new.

"Thanks," he said. He went to the hanger for his belt, pistol, and cap. I must have been very pale; my shirt felt soaked. Torres finished adjusting the buckle, straightened his pistol in the holster, and after automatically smoothing down his hair, he put on the cap. From his pants pocket he took out several coins to pay me for my services and then headed for the door.

In the doorway he paused for a moment and said, "They told me that you'd kill me. I came to find out. But killing isn't easy. You can take my word for it." And he turned and walked away.

THE GENERAL MAKES
A LOVELY CORPSE
Enrique Anderson Imbert

It is likely that Enrique Anderson Imbert was one of the first twentieth-century Argentine authors to write and publish detective stories in his country. He has few predecessors, and among them only the name of the nineteenth-century biologist-author E. L. Holmberg is remembered today. Anderson was also writing intellectual tales of fantasy in Argentina years before his compatriot Jorge Luis Borges composed his first metaphysical and philosophical fantasies. Like most of the "educated" Argentine authors of detective fiction, Anderson takes a satirical or sophistic view of the genre. This can be seen in nearly all of his detective stories and is evident in his keenly satirical "The General Makes a Lovely Corpse," wherein he combines comment on the political ills of his native country with a brilliant variation on the challenging "perfect crime" theme so frequently encountered in detective literature. Anderson, who has taught in Argentine universities as well as at the University of Michigan, is now Victor S. Thomas Professor of Hispanic American Literature at Harvard University. He is a prominent critic and historian of the literature of all of the Spanish American nations, and with his encouragement and direction the documentation of the development of detective literature in the Americas has been accomplished and this genre has come to receive acceptance in academic circles.

The General Makes A Lovely Corpse
E N R I Q U E   A N D E R S O N   I M B E R T

IN a place in South America the name of which I do not wish
to recall there lived not long ago a surgeon of fifty, so wealthy
he had no need to work. In his leisure time, which was most of
the year, he was given to reading detective stories. He plunged
himself so deeply into his reading that he spent whole nights
reading from sunset to sunrise and whole days reading from
dawn to dusk; and so, from little sleep and much reading, his
brain withered so that he lost his sanity. His imagination became filled with all he had been reading in books; and he came
up with the strangest thought ever had by any madman in the
world, which was that, annoyed because in all the novels he
read justice always ended by discovering the criminal, he decided
to commit a crime so perfect that he, its author, would never be
discovered.

Alfonso Quiroga—that was our hero's name—was strong of
body and agile of leg, but his head made him look prematurely
old: balding, wrinkled, with thick glasses and a big gray mustache. He lived on a beautiful estate, outside the city, his only
company that of his servants. In front rose two chalets. Apparently twins—inside, the arrangement of rooms was different—
they were separated by the garage, wide enough for three
automobiles. In the chalet on the left, which was where previously he had practiced his profession, Quiroga was installed.
The one on the right had remained uninhabited since his sisters
died. At the end of the garden, in a little white-washed house,
lived Bonifacia, an Indian woman now very old but irreplaceable
as cook, and Bonifacia's children: Lucía, shapely and charming;
Manuel, his mouth disfigured by a horse's kick; and his wife

151

Teresa, a faded woman. Still farther back, behind the little house, was a thatched hut, occupied by two *peons*.

Servants and *peons* respected the money and the kindness of Doctor Quiroga, although they were often irritated at seeing him so prone to meddle in the work of the estate. He was as apt to set about pruning the fruit trees in the orchard as to mobilize his chemical apparatus for the extermination of pests, or paint a fence, or go to the henhouse and twist the neck of a chicken for lunch. It was part of the physical exercise he had prescribed for himself so as not to succumb to a sedentary life. He did it, too, for love of country things. He would even go to the kitchen and help Bonifacia with the pastries, *tamales,* and meat turnovers! But nothing pleased him so much as reading the mystery stories he would receive by mail, direct from New York. It was precisely while reading *Dead and Not Buried* that, annoyed by the imaginative penury of H. F. M. Prescott, it occurred to Quiroga that not only would he be capable of writing a better novel, but even that he could do away with someone without there being any detective in the world who could unmask him.

He went up to his room, sat on the balcony—it was that time of the twilight when one still cannot see the stars but can hear them coming at full gallop—and amused himself by formulating a theory of the perfect crime. First condition, of course, that no one, in the last analysis, could find out who was the murderer. Nor why he killed. Nor how he killed. Nor with what he killed. But that was not enough. After all, crimes like this are a dime a dozen. A dozen? Ha! That's nothing. Ninety percent, he would say, ninety percent of such crimes escape the action of justice. They are, generally, blind crimes, counterfeit, clumsy, stupid. Truculencies. Atrocities. Offal of all the cities. Bah! Filth of outlaws and criminals. No. A perfect crime is, must be, an intellectual adventure. It requires the precise contexture of a charade. That's it! It has to be a masterpiece. A crime as rigorous and imaginative as a sonnet. That is the idea. And, like pure poetry, it must be unmotivated. To kill for profit, for vengeance, for jealousy, for fear, for politics, for misanthropy, for euthanasia, and so on, ruins the artistic possibilities of that neat act of cutting, gratuitously, the thread of life of one's fellow man. Kill for the pleasure of killing? Nor that either. Homicidal mania, no; maniacs not only cannot choose between good and evil, but they tend to backslide and end by repeating themselves. A perfect crime has to be free and unique. It is perpetrated without motive, without egotism. The perfect murderer must proceed in a sportsmanlike mood, in cold blood, like one who accepts a bet. Hitting some poor fellow on the head with a club as he walks along an alley in the dark is something thousands of malefactors can do: generally the police never find them. The decorous thing is to kill with style, impressing such a personal seal that it implies the risk of being caught. Here was the sportsmanlike part of the affair: sign the crime and nonetheless get away. Let the removal of a fellow man be beautiful in itself, like a sleight of hand. So as to increase that beauty it was proper to create difficult problems. For example: the problem of a corpse in a room locked from the inside, the problem of a corpse that disappears in the presence of many witnesses, the problem of a corpse that does not reveal the real but unimaginable weapon that fabricated it . . . And other, lesser problems: that of a series of murders committed in accordance with a secret key; that of the criminal who notifies the police as to how and when he will perpetrate his homicide; that of the alibi, false but indestructible; that of the tracks which are interrupted midway, with no apparent cause; that of the unfindable house; that of a ubiquitous man . . . And these problems had to be solved with trigonometric elegance. Quiroga gave a roguish little laugh. Trigonometry. How nice! The triangle of the victim, the murderer, and the detective.

Night had fallen, and now in the clouds could be seen the ominous glow of the city lights. Thousands and thousands of stars; and there below, thousands and thousands of beings who at that very instant would be coming and going through the labyrinth of streets. One of those beings would be the one chosen for sacrifice. One. Any one. Man, woman? It made no difference. He would choose the victim at random. Or rather, chance would choose the victim. How? Well . . . he could throw the telephone

153

book in the air so that it would fall open at any page whatever; he could, with his eyes closed, stick the point of a pencil over some name . . . No, no. The telephone book only gives the roll of one social sector, mostly masculine. Was it fair to disqualify as possible martyrs those who do not figure there, only because they cannot afford the luxury of a telephone or because the telephone is in the name of the head of the family? No indeed. One must complicate the game of chance. In order to correct the undemocratic nature of the telephone book he resorted to saints whose feast days are commemorated every day of the year. Let the telephone book indicate the surname, and the sanctoral cycle indicate the given name. He tore the pages off the calendar on the wall and scrambled the days in the wastebasket. He put his arm in and drew out the little page for the 19th of March: San José. Then he made a slip of paper for each letter of the alphabet. He scrambled them. He drew one: the "M." Things were moving along: "Jose M————." On other slips of paper he wrote only the numbers of these pages of the telephone book which included the subscribers with the letter M. He scrambled them. He drew one: page 387. He wrote a number for each line: he drew the number 9. Anxiously, holding his breath, he made his fingers descend along the tower of surnames. The surname on the ninth line of the second column on page 387 was Melgarejo. Except that there was no José Melgarejo there. All right. It didn't matter. He would look for him. First thing in the morning, he would go out hunting. He laughed as though someone were tickling him. Fine hunting! First, he would hunt the victim; afterwards, a detective would try to hunt him. Ha, ha! Not bad, not bad! "José Melgarejo." Thirteen fateful letters. Who would it be? He went to bed. He slept the sleep of the just: one of his dreams was that José Melgarejo did not exist.

Because—need it be said?—Quiroga was deceiving himself. If it was a question purely and simply of dispatching a man to the other world, why such cabala? Just be casting a glance at some Tom, Dick, or Harry of flesh and blood, it could be all done. Wouldn't that be better? Ah! The fact was that there, in the deepest cave of his soul, was Quiroga's other ego, hoping the apocryphal José Melgarejo would keep on being very much apocryphal. But Quiroga deceived himself. He was satisfied. Chance had formed a name: if Chance did not also form a man, it would not be his fault. When he saw there was no José Melgarejo in the phone book he felt relieved, although he pretended not to. Why did he discard the idea of going to the Civil Register and enquiring, once and for all, whether or not there was such a person as José Melgarejo? He persuaded himself that it was so that the trail of his curiosity would not betray him. But the hidden reason was another: he was afraid of finding that indeed this gentleman did live.

However it might be, the truth is that Quiroga embarked on the preparations for the perfect crime. How, when, where, and with what, he still could not know. When he came across the victim he would think about all that. With the threads of the circumstances he would weave his plot. In the meantime, the first thing he had to do was to burn his detective library, so that no one could go nosing around there and smell the pie. And then, encircle his life with a halo of innocence. Still better, turn his whole life into a colossal alibi. Without exaggerating, without attracting attention with unaccustomed behavior, he had to heighten his reputation—stainless, to tell the truth—so that, whatever might happen, no one would dare accuse him. Belonging to the Creole ruling class was a help to him. He was esteemed in influential social circles as a good conservative, rich, cultured, and law-abiding. (His madness was interior and secret.) If he let anything show it was mere eccentricity. But who was going to notice? At that time the whole country was topsy-turvy, and day by day the simpletons were willing to believe anything at all; who, then, would wonder at the opinions Quiroga gave out from his armchair at the Club? Inoffensive opinions, at that. And his newspaper articles? Judge the subjects: folklore, genealogy, patriotic anecdotes . . . Nothing more to be said: he was respected. There were even district politicians who were considering the possibilities of Doctor Quiroga as Nationalist Party candidate. Quiroga smiled. He a politician? What an idea!

Never, never. But he preened himself with pleasure. His respectability added a new wicked satisfaction to his macabre fantasies: if he were caught after murdering, he would fall like Samson, his arms around the pillars of society.

One afternoon the big city resounded with the cavalry of the army marching on Government House. Hours later it was announced over the radio that a junta of military men, presided over by General Veintemilla, would govern provisionally to save the country for I no longer remember what evils. The Nationalists cheered the army, offered the General their support, and solicited public posts. Then the self-effacing soul of Doctor Quiroga was more admirable than ever. He gave advice, went to party gatherings, brought people together, wrote editorials for the official newspaper, but modestly obscured himself. Again: a self-effacing soul. "If you wish, doctor . . ." Not a chance. The doctor did not wish. He wished nothing. He would never accept a salaried job from the government.

Unexpectedly there sprung up a new leader: a general who had just returned from Mussolini's Italy after several years as military attaché in the Embassy. In secret he organized the regimental commanders and one morning the papers brought the news with full-page headlines: "Veintemilla Resigns"; "New Junta Names General José Melgarejo President."

His heart gave such a leap that Quiroga thought someone else was living in his body. Also his head was spinning, and in one spin he was on the point of finding the sanity he had lost. José Melgarejo! He looked at himself in the mirror. Changed. Circles under his eyes. They looked at each other, he and his reflection, and said to each other with the same movement of the lips, "So he *has* appeared." He was ashamed of being pusillanimous and, with the recklessness of a fanatic, hurled himself towards the adventure. He had to plan the crime. The first step: approach the victim.

It was not difficult. He even allowed himself the luxury of refusing, several times, the invitations of the Nationalists to visit the dictator. Finally he accepted and met him at a closed meeting of military men and politicians. José Melgarejo was short of stature, with tiny hands, very soft flesh, and a certain feminine plumpness, but his face revealed in every glance the ascendancy of a leader. Quiroga, however, did not feel the magnetism of those glances: from the first instant he saw him already dead, with eyes closed. He certainly did make a lovely corpse! Quiroga took part wisely in the conversation. They invited him to other meetings. And in the hysteria of those days his words sounded sane. Quiroga's seriousness looked like patriotism: it was really the rigidity of the schemer. He delighted Melgarejo. Once Melgarejo invited him alone. They talked about the crisis. The military government had been discredited: how to make it popular? Quiroga proposed that, in one form or another, money be given to everybody. Ingenious. Formidable. Nobody had thought of it. And if he, Melgarejo, were to broadcast over the Government Radio a speech announcing the good news? Yes, it would be a good beginning. Doctor Quiroga, by all means, would have to take it upon himself to write the speech. Good. Yes. Doctor Quiroga would write it.

And so Quiroga had access to the dictator's office and soon was completely at home there. He did not accept the offer of a General Directorship, a display of modesty which gained for him still more of the esteem of Melgarejo. They became friends. Sometimes Melgarejo invited Quiroga to his home. Sometimes it was Quiroga who took him to enjoy one of those delicious dinners Bonifacia knew how to prepare. One night, having dinner at Quiroga's house, Melgarejo showed grave concern over the growing strength of the opposition.

"One must give appearances of legality to the acts of the government," Quiroga advised. "It would be best to call for elections and you become constitutional president."

"What if they don't elect me?"

"Of course they'll elect you! You know how these things are done. Nothing to worry about. The opposition is held in check. A tiny bit of fraud . . . At worst, you stay, whatever happens, and everything remains as it is now."

The election campaign was organized. Quiroga was with Melgarejo at all times. He was constantly giving proofs of his loyalty.

157

He shielded him with his body when the train in which he was traveling was assaulted by gunmen. He pulled his chestnuts out of the fire when some army leaders began to mutiny. The politicians, sure that Doctor Quiroga harbored no personal ambitions (and that, on the other hand, he did not oppose the personal ambitions of the others), aided him. There were reluctant leaders, in the most distant provinces.

"Leave them to me," said Quiroga. "I'll invite them to my house. A native *fiesta,* with wine, meat turnovers, roast lamb, filled cookies, and . . . folklore! You make them a little speech. They'll go back to their districts vibrating with patriotic enthusiasm. Leave them to me."

On the eve of the *fiesta*—Saturday—Melgarejo and Quiroga spent the whole afternoon in Government House. They went out at nightfall. In the anteroom they were joined by the aide-de-camp, Major Rosas. "Ah, the aide-de-camp is also coming to spend the night with me," Quiroga said to himself. "Very well: instead of following Plan 1, I shall follow Plan 2 or Plan 3, whichever is more appropriate." They got into the presidential car and departed. The city, always nightwalking, was awakening and opening thousands and thousands of illuminated eyes. But in the suburbs the park, dark as a single patch of trees, had lain down and seemed to be sleeping with one eye open: the lake. They left the park behind. At the sides of the road, a few humble houses. Then, country. Another group of houses, with a little baroque church praying in the night, and in five minutes they reached Doctor Quiroga's estate. They passed through the gates, dismissed the chauffeur, and went into the main chalet. They had dinner. Quiroga brought some papers and made ready to take notes on the next day's party.

"You may retire when you like," the General said to his aide-de-camp. "Doctor Quiroga and I will be working late. Tomorrow, at eleven—no: at half past eleven, come to ask for orders."

"Ah," interceded Quiroga with the shy air of the host who is afraid of not offering his guests all the comfort to which they are entitled, "in the other chalet I have only one room ready; so, if you don't mind, both of you stay here. The Major can sleep

158

in my room. Allow me to show you the way. Your room, General, is all ready. When we are through working I'll go to the other chalet."

"By no means," said Melgarejo. "The Major can sleep in the other chalet and we stay here. Why should you give up your own room? I wouldn't think of letting you do that! The Major will be comfortable there, won't he?"

"Of course," answered the Major.

"As you wish," said Quiroga. And he thought, "It's necessary, then, to follow Plan 3."

They said good night. Quiroga and Major Rosas left the chalet, went past the garage, and entered the twin chalet. After seeing the Major to his room, Quiroga rejoined the General and they began to exchange ideas. Quiroga was taking notes and hiding his impatience. Half an hour more and—the perfect crime! He had envisioned the most minor details. Plan 3. Each thing, in its place. The time of each action, calculated minute by minute. The movements of the people, foreseen even in their incongruities. His alibi, infallible. In his imagination he had gone through every stage of the murder, in his imagination he had already murdered. He knew what precautions to take in each case so as not to leave traces. Now, before really murdering, he contemplated in his mind, for the last time, the diagram of that game. Impeccable. Exact. Nothing was missing, not even the challenge to the police. For at the end he had left an enormous unknown. More gentlemanly he could not be. Fair play. There that loose end remained, to spur the interest of some policeman. In the annals of the police would be inscribed that golden question mark.

When the servants and *peons* withdrew to the little servants' house and the thatched hut, lost in the depths of the garden—it was half past nine—they saw the chalet lighted. Someone was still working there.

Sunday. Seven o'clock in the morning. Bonifacia, when she got up, found Doctor Quiroga in the patio, hanging from a garland a huge portrait of General Melgarejo. The portrait, smiling, looked like the advertisement for some dentifrice.

159

"He's nice, the General, isn't he?" said Bonifacia.

"Yes, isn't he?"

"Is he still sleeping?"

"Like a log."

"Shall I get breakfast?"

"For me? No, thank you. I've already had it. In a little while I'll go and see if Major Rosas is awake. If he is, I'll tell you, and you can ask Lucía to take him his breakfast. Watch out for Lucía! Heh, heh! The major must have a good eye for pretty girls . . . Don't worry about the General. He's going to sleep late. There's a lot to do. Have Manuel kill the lamb and light the fire. Don't you lose sight of him. Remember, today we're staking our reputation as cooks! The sauce: Bonifacia, careful with the sauce! Ah. I've already tried one of the filled cookies: do you know they turned out beautifully? And the dough for the meat turnovers, I don't have to tell you. It looks good. Let's hope the filling matches it. After you try it, tell me in all frankness, how you like it. Now go and fill the turnovers. What about Teresa?"

"She went to Mass."

"Good. When she comes back, have her dress nicely, in the dress I brought her. The same with Lucía. Have them set the table. Another thing: don't let Lucía get my guests excited, eh? Heh, heh! The girl has the devil in her flesh. I will tell you, Bonifacia, what time the fat has to begin heating. When the musicians get here have someone give them some glasses of wine. And what else? Very well, that's all for now. Go ahead."

Behind the chalet, between the garden and the fountain, they arranged the chairs for the musicians. The patio narrowed, entered into a summerhouse covered with native jasmine—there they set out the tables—and went out the other side, to widen again on its way to the garden. The peons came and celebrated the sacrifice of the roast lamb. Teresa came and put on the peasant skirt—yellow and rose—Doctor Quiroga had ordered. The musicians and dancers came and disguised themselves in more or less traditional costumes. Finally Lucía came, with her brand new skirt—violet and yellow. Major Rosas—ocher, red,

160

silver, gold, black, green, blue—appeared, very satisfied, twisting his mustache, and added to the native carnival touches of Viennese operetta.

"Doctor Quiroga," he said, "it's time now. I'm going to ask the General for orders."

"The General? I haven't seen him yet. Is it eleven already?"

"Half past eleven."

They went to the guest room. Quiroga knocked at the door, respectfully. No one answered. Now he knocked hard. Nothing. He turned to Major Rosas and told him, laughing:

"It took effect for him! Last night he couldn't sleep. He took a sleeping pill. Shall we wake him?"

But they couldn't open the door.

"General!" shouted the Major. He shook the door. He shouted again, putting his mouth to the keyhole. He tried to look through the keyhole.

"It's locked from the inside," said the Major.

"Yes, I see it is," answered Quiroga. And he added, laughing again, "Do you hear how he's snoring? We won't wake him even with cannon shots!"

And in fact one could hear the sleeper's breathing, deep, slow, rhythmic.

"There's no other door?"

"No. But the room has a window, facing the patio. Let's try."

They went along the corridor, came out onto a porch—from where one could see the patio and the summerhouse—and approached the window. It was closed, the catches locked from the inside. A thick curtain, drawn, allowed nothing to be seen in the interior of the room.

"It doesn't matter," said Quiroga. "There's a skylight in back, but it's very high and, besides, so small we couldn't get our heads through it. There's nothing to be done. Let's wait. We can let him sleep another hour. If he doesn't get up when the guests arrive"—and he laughed again—"we'll batter the door down, knock him around, and give him a shower. He must have taken more than the dose of narcotic I prescribed for him."

Five after twelve. Three automobiles arrived, filled with people.

161

The girls began serving the vermouth. The guitars and bass drums burst out playing *vidalas, cuecas, zambas*. Groups of very animated conversation formed. Quiroga apologized for not being able to be with all of them. He kept going from one side to another, smiling, attentive. Now and then he would go into the house, but the guests didn't miss him. Now came another round of vermouth, served by the lovely Lucía. Quarter to one. The dancers formed for the *cueca*. At last, Quiroga went up to the Major and said:

"So? How's it going? Do you like the dancers?"

"Very much," answered the Major. And he added, after a silence, "You still haven't seen the General?"

"No. He must still be sleeping."

"Don't you think we should go and tell him everyone has arrived?"

"Yes, you're right. How stupid of me! What time is it?"

"Quarter after one."

"Already? How awful! How the time does go! Yes, of course. The General has to be called. Shall we go?"

Turning, Quiroga raised his eyes and looked towards the General's window.

"Yes. He's up," he told the Major, pointing to it. "Don't you see? He's opened the curtains."

They reached the room, knocked. No one answered. The Major leaned against the doorknob and the door gave way. Except that, when it opened, the General was not there. The bed, unmade; the sheets, rumpled; the pillow, dented. In the keyhole, the key. Apparently, the General had dressed and gone out of the bedroom. Nor did they find him in the bathroom. Bonifacia —the only one who, aside from Doctor Quiroga, had been going in and out of the house—knew nothing.

"Where can he have gone?" murmured Quiroga. "Unless . . ."

"Unless. . . ?" repeated the Major.

"Nothing. I'll tell you later."

Quiroga took the Major by the arm and they went through other parts of the house. No. The General had made an exit. They went out to the front garden. Nothing. The chauffeur was

162

waiting there now with the presidential car. No, the chauffeur had not seen the General.

"How strange!" exclaimed the Major. "Where can he have gone to?"

"It might be that while we were coming in the back way, he was going out the front. Who knows; maybe he has already joined the guests. Let's go."

"Where can he have gone to?" murmured the Major.

"Could he have gone to Mass?" asked Quiroga, without conviction.

"To Mass? I doubt it.... You said, 'Unless ...' "

"Nothing, nothing. We'll talk about it later. Now the guests have to be attended to. We'll act as if the General has had to leave because of an urgent matter. Chances are he'll be back in time."

Half past one. They sat down at the table. Bonifacia and the girls brought platters full of meat turnovers just taken from the pan. The wine began to flow. "Long live General Melgarejo!" "*Viva, viva!*" The frugal Quiroga went to see if the roast was done and, in passing, asked the musicians to play a *carnavalito*. After the meat turnovers, the lamb. And later, filled cookies, fruit . . . The Major looked at Quiroga and made a sign to him: "So? What do we do now?" Now it was impossible to wait any longer. The dancers had finished. The dishes had been cleared away. Bonifacia was bringing the coffee. Doctor Quiroga stood up, waited for silence, and began his speech. He apologized for the involuntary absence of General Melgarejo and at once intoned praises. With voluptuous mischief he chose his words in such a way that they served simultaneously as panegyric and funeral oration. Nobody perceived his necrological subtleties, and Quiroga smiled on hearing the shouts, now useless indeed, of "Long live the General!" "*Viva, viva!*" Other speeches resounded, each more eloquent than the last. The after-dinner speeches ended. The fiesta was over. Everyone left. Everyone except Major Rosas.

"You must be exhausted, Doctor Quiroga; but will you allow me to abuse your hospitality a little longer?"

163

"Goodness! No trouble at all. Whatever you wish. You're most welcome."

"Thank you. I'd like to make a telephone call, to see if the General is at home or has gone to Government House."

No. No one knew where the General was.

"Doesn't it seem strange to you?" asked the Major as he re-placed the receiver. "I just can't understand how the General can have gone away like that, without saying good-bye to anybody, without even telling you . . . I remember you were about to say something . . . 'Unless . . .' you began to say, and stopped. What were you going to say?"

"Very well. The General himself, when you see him, will ex-plain to you better than I can why he left. It was because, last night, after many hours of writing and tearing up papers, he felt irritated. Suddenly the idea of this *fiesta* annoyed him. . . . I don't know . . . He got the idea that it was humiliating for him to have to lower himself to this . . . That he had no reason to go looking for the friendship of the politicians . . . That, after all, he was governing by the strength of the army and had no need of electoral farces . . . And he even hinted that, like as not, he'd go away without waiting for anybody. And moreover, that he was so tired of struggling with problems that couldn't be solved, that he felt like sending the whole thing to the devil, quitting the government, and going off to some quieter place, to play golf or simply sit in the park . . . Those are his words. I laughed. I didn't contradict him. He was talking and talking. He was very excited. I suppose that's why he asked me for a sedative, to be able to sleep. Naturally, I didn't believe him. But the rest of it you already know; when we opened the door and saw that the General had gotten up and gone off without a word I suspected that he had made good his threat."

"But if that's the way it is, where did he go? And how? He had no car, so he had to go on foot. Set off down the road, on foot, at noon? Hmm! I don't think so."

"And if he walked to the church? And from there to the park?"

"I don't like to say this, Doctor Quiroga, but I don't think so.

164

Well, we just have to wait. There's something strange about it. If you don't mind I'd like to take another look at the General's bedroom."

They went. It had not yet been straightened. The Major observed everything. On the night table, a lamp plugged in to an outlet in the baseboard, and the bottle with the sleeping pills. In the wall opposite the door there was a small skylight, partly open. The curtains, opened; but the window was locked.

The Major came back the following day.

"I'm afraid there's been foul play," he told Quiroga after informing him that the General had not appeared anywhere. "A kidnapping. A crime. I don't know."

"Yes. Something serious has happened," Quiroga agreed, very worried. "Because you don't think he may have had some kind of breakdown, of amnesia, and escaped from here . . ."

"No, how could I think that. Do you?"

"Frankly, no."

"Very well. To work, then. Will you let me inspect the whole estate, question the servants? It's not that I want to play Sherlock Holmes . . ."

In Quiroga's imagination the mention of the magic name Sherlock Holmes had the virtue of conferring upon Major Rosas the faculties of Sherlock Holmes himself. Sherlock Holmes, the miracle man, reincarnated and at work again. "Ah," he said to himself, "Major Rosas is one of my own." He was not expecting the detective to appear so soon. Nor that it would be a detective with an aura of novels. There were all sorts of detectives: drug addicts, cynics, blind ones, detectives with skirts, with cassocks, doctors, newspaper men, lawyers, art critics . . . How nice! The collection was being completed: an army major detective . . . And, pleased, he divined in the lynx eyes of Major Rosas a genius for analysis and deduction. Now one would see whether the methods of Sherlock Holmes were infallible.

Monday. Major Rosas invited Quiroga to accompany him to Government House. The junta, assembled to consider the emergency, wanted to hear him. Quiroga, without turning a hair, gave all the information they asked of him. Yes, he said, it is possible that it may be a kidnapping. If the General went on foot as far as the church, it is likely that an opposition group watching our house picked him up in an automobile. In the best of cases, they will have locked him up somewhere.

The Chief of Police, who was present, was listening as though to rain falling. Quiroga was alarmed at his negligence.

Tuesday. Three in the afternoon. In Government House the members of the junta, the Chief of Police, Major Rosas, and Doctor Quiroga, meeting again. The question is a burning one. The General has gone up in smoke. And if the opposition finds out? How long can they keep the secret? Doctor Quiroga suggests that the police go to his house, go over the ground inch by inch, question everyone present at the *fiesta* . . . Yes, this will be done and even more, says one of the military men; and turning to the Chief of Police he orders him:

"You yourself, personally, take charge of the investigation for me, eh?"

The Chief of Police stands at attention, takes his cap, his saber, and says to Quiroga:

"Shall we go, doctor?"

"Let's go," answers Quiroga; and turning to Major Rosas he tries to commit him with a "Shall we go?" so that he too can go with th̄ n and not lose the scent. Because, Quiroga has thought, Major Rosas, no one else, must be the Detective. The Chief of Police? A blockhead. An incompetent. He'll dash to the ground the beautiful castle built in the air. The Major, on the other hand, has acumen. He alone is capable of putting one clue inside another and using the logical apparatus like a telescope. One flaw, one simple flaw in the crime, and the Major would notice it and end by clearing up the enigma. If he did not clear it up, what better tribute to Quiroga's masterliness? Proudly, Quiroga was challenging the most capable one. One intelligence against another intelligence, this is what was still missing from the novel he was living. For that reason he invited the Major, the connoisseur, the bloodhound. And the Major went.

But what Quiroga feared, happened. The next day the Chief of Police, clumsily overdoing his zeal, began arresting politicians of the opposition, breaking into the places where they were plotting. On his advice, the army did the same with some anti-Melgarejo officers. And, as is natural, the country found out this way that something was up. Before the week was out everyone knew that General Melgarejo had disappeared. The opposition came out in the open. Revolutionary handbills were distributed. Walls were papered with posters against the government. There were strikes. The students vociferated. Shots. Deaths. A sector of the army took advantage of the confusion to make a coup d'état. The new dictator, General Villa, announced from the balconies of Government House that the regime of Melgarejo had rotted; that it was necessary to amputate and that now the country was out of danger. The people were shouting: "Long live General Villa!" Someone in a café insinuated quietly that like as not General Villa had had General Melgarejo eliminated. Another gave the conjecture as truth. A third added that actually it had been a duel. There were variants. It had not been a duel with sabers, but with pistols. It had not been a duel, but an act of courage: Villa entered Government House all alone, pushed his way through, and liquidated Melgarejo with one finger, the trigger finger. General Villa became a national hero. Flattered, he denied nothing, said nothing. Overnight Major Rosas was exiled to the Embassy in Madrid, which confirmed the legend that General Villa had shot Melgarejo. Why, otherwise, send away the aide-de-camp? The police thought it prudent to bury the affair. So as not to touch off by chance, in handling the thing, an explosive. The disappearance of General Melgarejo became a state secret. The newspapers didn't dare even to mention it. When General Villa proclaimed the amnesty, his supporters interpreted it as a Law of Forgetting and believed they knew what it was that Villa wanted them to forget. People, therefore, forgot Melgarejo.

Quiroga was indignant. "Cheaters! That's not the way to play, damn it!" In the first place, they were despoiling his crime of the glory of an investigation. That was not fair. The police were giving up before the puzzle was formed. Tricksters! The wit of a murder is in defeating, with good sportsmanship, following the

167

rules, the best efforts of the police. But if the police, at the very outset, were abandoning the case, what had been the use of the murderer's delicacy? What a stupid country! Nowhere else would the police withdraw from the gaming table leaving the murderer sitting comfortably, with the aces in his hand. Closing the Melgarejo case amounted to throwing a jewel in the trash, together with a quantity of ordinary crimes that are never solved, not because they are unsolvable, but because of the indifference of the authorities. And perhaps at that very hour Major Rosas was going around boasting that, if he hadn't been sent out of the country, he would have solved the mystery. Yes, it's possible that Major Rosas had some suspicion. Why not? That wonderful sleight of hand with Melgarejo's body had to attract suspicions. He had counted on their suspecting him. He was even proud of their suspecting him. But would Major Rosas have been capable of finding some loose thread in the sumptuous tapestry of his crime? No, it was not possible. Quiroga was sure of his art. How amusing it would have been to confront the suspicions of Major Rosas and deflate them—pim, pam, poom— with pinpricks! Unverifiable suspicions. Perhaps, in many, many years, when he felt himself dying, he would call that Sherlock Holmes with saber, insignia, and rank bars, and play with him like a cat with a mouse. "Do you remember that day of the *fiesta*," he would say at last, now with one foot in the stirrup, and after having humiliated him, "do you remember when you and I went up to the guest room? Very well: General Melgarejo did not exist then even as a *corpus delicti*." "Really? It can't be! Do you mean to tell me the General did not die in bed? What! I thought . . ." "I know, I know . . . Generals, normally, die in bed; but General Melgarejo never got to bed. I rumpled the bed, to make it look as though he had slept there." "And the snores we heard?" "Bah! Produced by a tape recorder. The room, my friend, was unoccupied." "But it was locked from the inside!" Major Rosas would say, without coming out of his stupor. Quiroga would smile at him pityingly. "Elementary, my dear Rosas, elementary." And he would tell him how he left the skylight open but locked the window, went out of the room, locked the door from the outside and took out the key, went around the room by the corridor, leaned against the back wall, stuck the key into the crack of a bamboo pole, from the skylight reached across the room with the pole, and put the key in the inside of the keyhole. Rosas, open-mouthed and without dissembling his admiration, would exclaim, "Now I understand: with the same deceits, only proceeding in reverse, you took back the key and opened the door to make me think Melgarejo had gone out of the room. Doctor: you are a genius! Of course, nobody missed you, because the *fiesta* was going on in the patio and the guests found it quite natural that you would move about. . . . Doctor: you are a genius." "Thank you, dear friend; now you will understand why, in order to keep the secret of that masterly crime I have just now confessed to you, I have to kill you. That small glass of anise brandy you drank was poisoned. I'm sorry." Quiroga sighed. A genius? Well . . . why deny it? He was a genius, in effect. But his ingenious edifice was now crumbling. Not only had they snatched away from him the satisfaction of measuring his strength with justice and defeating it, but they had even stolen his murder. Yes, General Villa was a thief. He had stolen all his fame. Probably he was an upstart incapable of killing a fly. And there he was in the presidential chair, playing the peacock in borrowed plumage, like a hero of South American history painted with the fascinating colors of blood. Not only that: Villa, in stealing his crime, debased it. Quiroga had consummated it with no ill will, with all purity and disinterestedness; in the eyes of public opinion, however, that homicide ended up reduced to tyrannicide. Such was his resentment that he even had the impulse to go to the Plaza Central and shout to the four winds: "The murder is mine! I, I, I alone am the murderer!" And they would arrest him. And he would carefully dictate his confession. And the next day, in the newspapers, with big headlines, they would publish it. The expression of the *señoras!* It made one laugh just to imagine their looks of distaste. Because in the good detective stories, even in those that are not good literature, the passion for abstract problems imposes a frozen reserve upon the description of the

169

slaughter. Those novels never go so far as to give repugnance. But the most dispassionate style of the newspaper account makes the reader's sensations boil in a red bath. Newspapers can indeed give repulsion. "No sooner had Major Rosas retired to the other chalet," one would read in *El Bien Público,* "than the ingenious Doctor Alfonso Quiroga administered an anaesthetic to Melgarejo and, when he lost consciousness, undressed him, applied tourniquets to his arms and legs to avoid abundant hemorrhage, laid him out in the bathtub, let the water run so as to carry away the blood before it coagulated and began to quarter him alive, with all his surgeon's skill. Melgarejo died in the course of the delicate surgical operation. He took out his innards, clipped off his head, and divided the body into four pieces. From the fleshiest parts he set aside a few pounds, neatly cut. The rest, wrapped in a waterproof cloth, he took to the kitchen, where he had set to heat, on the gas stove, a copper boiler filled with a solution of caustic soda and water. He boiled the head first and then, one by one, the members and loose pieces. As the proteins and fats dissolved he would take out the bones with tongs, wash them in the sink and splinter them. In a pan he heated nitric acid and there dissolved the bones: the smoke was going up the chimney. When he renewed the acid he was careful to mix it with plenty of water so that, when he poured it down the sink, it wouldn't rot the pipes. The clothing he disintegrated in the caustic soda solution. He cleaned the instruments and put them back in place. . . ." And so on. The face the readers of *El Bien Público* would put on! Even the black ink of the newspaper would have a deleterious smell. And the nocturnity of that scene! Sublime, sublime . . . What a great model! Classic.

But he would not confess. It would be madness. With a confession he would gain nothing. He would ruin the only merit remaining to him: that it would never be known who had killed Malgarejo, and how. Without taking into account that, if he confessed, chances are they would appoint him minister. For that's how things were going in his country: now not even a decent crime could be committed because immediately they made one a hero. What a pity! Such a pretty crime, so well done . . . The hecatomb of the new military revolution had taken from Melgarejo's disappearance the horror of death and the grace of playing with death. A vast conspiracy of politicians, military men, newspaper writers, policemen, charlatans, and cowards had invented a patriotic motive that dishonored the disinterestedness of the homicide. Blast them! Why are detective stories written in English? Could it be because only in civilized countries is there an aversion to violent death? Or can it be that all those detective stories are false? A mental game, false as that of the mathematician who traces his formula knowing that never will he come across anything like it, irresponsible as that of the chess player who, on a checkered board, checks a wooden piece. The criminal, in those novels, strives to close his crime like a locked room, with a chain of well-linked causes and effects. But that order—wasn't it false? Order necessarily separate from life. Life which is an absurd chaos. Now Quiroga despised those novels. He was glad to have burned them. He promised himself not to read even one more.

Little by little his spirits were calming down. And he consoled himself thinking that it was not his fault that the skillful gradation of his crime had ended in an anticlimax; with a push they made the crime roll down the stairs, to the basement, grotesquely. Yes, everything had come tumbling down, but God and he knew the crime had been perfect. A crime of sacred symbolism, with liturgical magnificences. The neatly cut pounds of flesh he had set aside he put through the meat grinder. He fried the ground meat, seasoned it, mixed it with hard-boiled eggs, olives, raisins. By then it was almost seven o'clock in the morning. He let Bonifacia fill the meat turnovers with that. The politicians, to the shouts of "Long live Melgarejo!", in a communion of mystic faith, ate Melgarejo in turnovers. What beauty, what beauty! Oh, if only there had been a criminologist worthy of such a crime! Beatifically, with resignation, Quiroga lifted his eyes to heaven. Something of that candid glow which, after the holocaust of Abel, must have lighted the face of Cain, shone also on the face of Quiroga. "God and I," he repeated, "know that, in spite of everything, the crime was perfect." And he offered to God, sole and mute spectator, his homicide round as a host.

Translated from the Spanish by Isabel Reade

THE DEAD MAN WAS A LIVELY ONE
Pepe Martínez de la Vega

Pepe Martínez de la Vega was one of Mexico's most popular humorists, and for years he wrote with great success for a series of comedy radio shows. There is a certain Mexican flavor to all of his work, to which his radio audience responded instinctively. When he turned to writing short stories and created Peter Pérez, it was inevitable that his detective would not be from the old school. The dignity of the detective story was destined to suffer a few pokes in the ribs, but everyone would end up having a good time. Sure enough, the Peter Pérez tales are one leg-pull after another. Consider his solution of a locked-room mystery that had positively baffled the Mexico City police. Called to the scene of the crime, Peter confirmed that the dead man had indeed been found in a locked room, with the windows locked and barred, no secret passages, no trap doors . . . An impossible crime. But not for Peter. "Elementary, my dear chaps," he observed calmly. "I have the solution. You will note that the room has no roof." Mexican critic María Elvira Bermúdez has aptly described the attitude that the author has conferred on his detective. "Peter Pérez is wise and gracious and always solves the crime, but his methods are broad caricatures of traditional detective-fiction techniques. With generous doses of popular humor, he effectively expresses the peculiarly Mexican scorn for everything that represents precision, fastidiousness, and routine." As you may observe in "The Dead Man Was a Lively One."

The Dead Man Was a Lively One

(An Adventure of Peter Pérez,
the Brilliant Detective
from Peralvillo)

P E P E   M A R T Í N E Z   D E   L A   V E G A

A MAN on a bicycle was pedaling through the darkened streets of the elegant residential district. His visored cap seemed to suggest he was a telegraph messenger and, as a matter of fact, that's what he was: a telegraph messenger.

After checking by a streetlight the name of the street he was on, the cyclist stopped in front of number 135 and approached the doorbell with the intention of submitting it to what union leaders submit workers to when it's time to collect dues: pressure.

After ringing for ten minutes, the messenger had just about given up all hope of delivering the telegram, when a woman appeared in the doorway of the luxurious mansion. She was young and very attractive. She took the message, signed for it, and tore open the envelope.

"It's for my husband," she said as she closed the door.

The messenger got on his bicycle and was just setting off again when the woman appeared at the door shouting, "Come back, come back!"

The messenger, whose name was José González Beck, politely removed his cap, saying, "At your service, *señora.*"

"Help! Help!" the lady exclaimed now.

"Ah, that's something else, *señora.* What's the trouble?"

"My husband has been murdered. Call the police."

The messenger put in a call to the police station and gave the address to Sergeant Juan Vélez who was then on duty.

175

A Horrible Sight

Detective Sergeant Juan Vélez at that moment was in his office chatting with the brilliant detective from Peralvillo, Peter Pérez.

In the company of the celebrated Peter, the Sergeant left for the fashionable home where the crime had been committed.

The victim's wife was the only occupant of the handsome mansion. The sight that Peter and the Sergeant beheld was horrible, as horrible, for example, as the marketplace of San Juan.

In the middle of the luxuriously furnished room lay the body of the man who in his lifetime was Saturnino Flores. A trickle of blood ran from an armchair to beneath a small ornamental table some twenty feet away. There was a dagger protruding from the back of the corpse. The dead man held a rose in his left hand and a bunch of flowers in the right. One of the fingers of his right hand was smeared with blood. Before dying, Saturnino had traced a strange circle with his own blood on the waxed floor.

The wife briefly related what had happened. She had been listening to the radio when she heard the doorbell. She went to answer and accepted the telegram for her husband. She read it and, though it was not a matter of great importance, decided to pass the news on to her husband immediately. On entering the room she discovered the body and quickly called the messenger who phoned the police. That was all.

Peter Pérez had been regarding the curious posture of the dead man. The Sergeant looked at the scene only briefly and then began to take notes.

"Your name, *señora?*" he said to the widow.

"Rosa Flores."

"What was your husband's business?"

"Sales manager."

At that instant, Peter Pérez, the brilliant detective from Peralvillo, interrupted the questioning to make a request:

"Would you be so kind as to lend me your husband's pen? I'd like to write a few things down and I didn't bring mine."

"My husband didn't have a pen," said the widow.

176

"Well, then, his pencil," suggested Peter.

"He didn't use a pencil either."

"Thank you so very much," replied Peter, with the elegant charm he always reserved for attractive women.

THE DEFEAT OF PETER PÉREZ

Sergeant Vélez saw the opportune moment and decided to act. Here, for the first time in his life, was the chance to defeat the great Peter in person.

Thus it was that, melodramatically, he exclaimed:

"You are under arrest, *señora,* for the murder of your husband."

The widow turned pale and murmured, "That's absurd!"

Sergeant Vélez dramatically strode to the telephone and called the editors of one of the morning newspapers, for he was very fond of publicity.

"In ten minutes," he said to the widow, "I shall explain to you my reasons for this decision. In the meantime, consider yourself under arrest."

And ten minutes later, in the presence of the representative of the press of Mexico City, Sergeant Vélez began his explanation.

"From the very outset," he said, "I realized that this woman was the murderer. There was no one else in the house, aside from the dead man, who happens to have a rose in his left hand and in his right a bouquet of flowers. Now, what was the reason for this strange whimsey on the part of a dying man? There is only one explanation: he wanted to indicate the identity of his assailant. The woman who stands here before us is named Rosa Flores.* As far as I am concerned, the case is as clear as if the dead man had left a letter ..."

"The dead man," exclaimed Peter, "could not possibly have left any sort of letter, because he was illiterate."

But Sergeant Vélez paid no attention and smiled with satisfaction as he basked amidst the admiring glances of his bootlicking subordinates.

* "Flores" in Spanish means "Flowers." (Translator's note.)

177

Peter Pérez held his silence. Vélez looked at him compassion-
ately, for he imagined that he had thoroughly outclassed him.

The Sergeant placed handcuffs on the wrists of the wretched
widow and the newspaper reporter was just about to take his
leave, when the great Peter spoke up.

"Just a moment. This woman did not kill her husband."

"Don't horn in, my friend," warned Vélez.

"I'm not horning in, Sergeant," replied the brilliant detective
coldly, "because I don't have a horn. I'm a rational being who
has merely a head."

"All right, then. Who killed Saturnino?" asked the newspaperman.

"I don't know yet. But what I am sure of is that it wasn't his
wife," said Peter. And he added: "Would you let me ask her a
few questions, Sergeant?"

"Go ahead. But make it quick," conceded Vélez reluctantly.
"I can't be wasting my time."

"Thank you. At what time, *señora,* did you retire to listen to
the radio?"

"At six o'clock P.M."

"How long after that did the telegram arrive?"

"It came at ten o'clock at night, four hours later. On account
of my husband's business schedule, we eat at five o'clock and
don't dine afterwards. I mean—" and she broke out sobbing,
"we used to eat then. Now I shall eat alone . . ."

"There, there, *señora,*" said Peter consolingly. "Try not to get
upset. Did your husband have any visitors today?"

"Yes, his business partner, *señor* Méndez, came to see him."

"What is Méndez's full name?"

"Juan B. Méndez," the woman replied. "They went into the
dining room. My husband offered him a drink, but *señor* Méndez
preferred to have coffee. I put out the electric coffeepot filled
with water and coffee enough for him to drink all he wanted."

"Where is the coffeepot, please? But first, do me the favor of
calling Méndez. I should like to talk with him."

"He's not at home. He should be back before long. He went
to the Iris Theatre to hear a speech by a political leader," said

178

the widow. "That's what he told my husband in my presence. He said that afterwards he'd return here. This is the coffeepot."

"It's empty," exclaimed the great detective from Peralvillo. "So it is . . ."

"How many cups of coffee could be made with the amount of water you provided?" Peter asked the woman.

"Seven."

"Thank you."

*　　*　　*

Moments later Juan B. Méndez arrived, visibly shaken by the fate that had befallen his friend and business associate.

Peter scarcely let him enter the room before he subjected him to an intense scrutiny and then asked him point blank:

"By any chance—please excuse the indiscretion—are you a relative of . . ."

". . . of Bouquet, the famous guitarist?" concluded Méndez in a slightly peevish tone. And then he replied, ill-humoredly, to his own question.

"No, sir. I've been hearing that question ever since I was in school."

"Excuse me, then. Where did you meet your late partner," asked Peter.

"In—in school, as a matter of fact."

"Where were you between six and ten o'clock this evening?"

"I left here around seven and went to the Iris Theatre to hear a speech by an important labor candidate. There are a thousand witnesses who can substantiate that . . ."

The medical examiner had now arrived and reported briefly to the sergeant that the victim had died between eight and nine o'clock that evening.

This interruption provided Sergeant Vélez with the excuse to put an end to the proceedings. He motioned to Peter and asked, "Are you finished now?"

"Yes. I've found out what I wanted," replied the brilliant detective from Peralvillo.

179

THE VICTORY OF PETER PÉREZ

And, quite nonchalantly, he added:

"This gentleman is also ready to go with you to Police Head-quarters." He indicated Méndez. "Arrest him, Sergeant. It was he who murdered his partner."

And then, to the astonishment of the newspaperman, the extraordinary detective, the pride of his neighborhood, explained:

"The first thing I became aware of was the fact that the dead man was a lively one. Because you have to be unusually shrewd to be illiterate and make such a comfortable living at the same time."

"Illiterate? Do you mean he couldn't read *or* write?" asked Vélez haltingly.

"Precisely, my friend. Precisely that. The business about his being a sales manager is pure fantasy. I have no doubt that what we're dealing with is top dog in the rackets hierarchy, some underworld chieftain's left hand man perhaps. Look at the furniture, look at the house, look at—the wife."

Peter cast an interested glance towards the widow and licked his lips.

"Get to the point, man! Stop beating around the bush!" demanded the Sergeant.

"The dead man, I repeat, was a lively number. On being mortally wounded by this individual, he searched desperately for some way to identify him. He didn't know how to write—an observation borne out by the absence of pens and pencils in this house as well as the fact that, when she received the telegram, his wife opened it for the purpose of reading it to him and certainly not out of lack of breeding. This woman has class. No, this merely shows that her husband couldn't have read it himself because he was illiterate. Gravely wounded, I repeat, he tried to find some way to leave a clue that pointed to his assassin and he remembered having heard that a zero on the left means nothing. He left it up to the intelligence of the police to see through his message. He took a rose in his left hand and drew the bloody circle to indicate that Rosa *was not* guilty, since by placing his left hand on the zero he showed that it meant nothing—zero on the left, you see. Then he took the fistful of flowers in his right hand to show us that they were an affirmation."

"Yes, but her name is Flores," said Vélez triumphantly.

"Of course, but he didn't mean to indicate 'flowers' alone. Notice that the flowers are in a solid cluster, in a bunch. From this I was able to deduce that the victim wanted to say *bouquet* and not flowers. His partner's name is surely not commonly Juan B. Méndez, but Juan Bouquet Méndez. Obviously, he suppressed the 'Bouquet' to throw the police off the track. Once a shifty character, always a shifty character, eh? He himself gave away his real name when he said that in school they used to ask if he were a relative of the guitarist Bouquet. Why would they ask him that? Simply because his name was Bouquet."

"Ah-ha! There I've caught you in a mistake, my good Peter," interrupted Vélez. "You said the victim was illiterate but at the same time he claims he met Méndez at school."

"Exactly, they met at school. Our friend Juan Bouquet Méndez was in school, but Saturnino wasn't. He was a *shoeshine boy*. This I discovered on examining the dead man's fingers, where there are unmistakable traces of shoe polish. He didn't shine his own shoes to save money, but simply out of habit . . . When he was a boy, Saturnino shined the shoes of the boys at school. It was there that he met 'Bouquet,' not 'Méndez,' the man who years later would be his killer. For Saturnino, Juan was always Bouquet and not Méndez. That was why he left the bouquet clue as part of his dying message."

"I have a perfect alibi," said Bouquet. "I was at the big political rally at the Iris. You can never prove all this . . ."

"You're wrong, my friend. I can prove it all," said Peter. "You were here before you left for the theatre and you drank seven cups of coffee in order not to fall asleep during the boring speech of the great leader of the masses. You were able to stay awake, but the others then fell asleep. You slipped out when they were all in dreamland. You committed the crime, getting into the house with a pass key you had secured earlier, and

181

then returned directly to the theatre where everyone was still dead asleep. They had all seen you arrive the first time, but no one saw you leave and return once more. You are very clever, but the dead man was even more so."

* * *

Juan B. Méndez confessed his guilt in the face of the convincing proof that Peter presented. The widow, overjoyed at being released, threw herself on Peter and gave him a kiss. Then, reconsidering her impulsiveness, she asked, with lowered eyes: "What do I owe you?"

"Nothing at all, *señora,*" replied Peter, flushed, but with delicate gallantry. "For me, a woman's kiss is worth more than all the treasure in the world."

And he departed with the modesty of all true geniuses. And without getting the kiss.

SHADOW OF A BIRD
Rodolfo J. Walsh

Rodolfo J. Walsh, as we noted on the introductory note to "Gambler's Tale," is probably the most professional of all Argentine detective-fiction writers. Critic, historian, anthologist, author of detective short stories and novelettes, and translator of North American detective novels, he is thoroughly familiar with all aspects of the genre. "Gambler's Tale" was a tidy, compact, ironic narrative developed around the original idea of a dice-player condemned to win. In the present longer story we see Walsh at work with a more conventional form, the on-the-scene investigation of a crime that leads logically to its solution. Around a single, cleverly handled clue, the author develops a fully rounded narrative that stands as a classic example of how to construct a "traditional" detective short story. Despite the fickle fluctuations of fashion, this type of detective tale is never out of style, indeed never has been since the first one of its type was conceived by Edgar Allan Poe in 1841 and given the inspired title of "The Murders in the Rue Morgue."

Shadow of a Bird

RODOLFO J. WALSH

CALMLY looking back on the sensational events of the Mariana Lerner affair—the one that bounced into the headlines of the Bueños Aires newspapers last summer—it now seemed to Daniel Hernández that the world had generously pardoned the girl. True—Mariana was beautiful. But she was also the victim, and the world, it seems, is always ready to pardon victims.

What other sanctions of her conduct the public might have conceded her it was not easy to say. But in spite of everything, in spite of the lurid details, Mariana will still be long remembered as beautiful.

Unfortunately, she didn't look it when Daniel Hernández and Inspector Jiménez first saw her. She was stretched out on the floor of the game room of her home, at the foot of one of her husband's many trophy cases. Her glistening blonde hair which had gladdened so many bright and noisy afternoons, so many receptions, which had inspired so many tender glances, now seemed opaque on the varnished wood of what was almost her last resting spot in this world. Her eyes were greatly dilated and her face was twisted into an odd grimace of pain or hate.

Two policemen were managing with difficulty to restrain Gregorio Altabe, the noted national sports figure—a huge, terrifying form—who was struggling to reach the body of his wife. Finally they succeeded in leading him to the adjoining room, and from there, for a while afterwards, could be heard his uncontrollable sobbing.

"This is starting off all wrong," said the inspector ominously. He stooped next to the dead woman and observed her through half-closed eyes. He put his index finger out cautiously and

185

touched the lifeless throat. Withdrawing the finger, he examined it closely, then turned to Daniel with a puzzled expression.

"Paint," he murmured.

Daniel looked at him, unblinking, through his glasses.

"Are you sure, Inspector? Then that must be more—there on her dress."

Jiménez bent down quickly to confirm the observation. It was true. On the white dress, near the shoulder, there was in fact an oddly irregular smudge of green paint in the fabric. At that moment, someone finally thought to turn on the overhead light. There then could be clearly seen overlaying the bluish prints of strangulation a set of green stains.

"I don't like it," murmured the inspector.

His men began to shift nervously. When Jiménez didn't like something he showed it with a crackling of orders. This instance was not the exception.

"Carletti. Cut off a piece of this material! Not there, idiot! Where it's painted! Now, off to the laboratory! Ramírez, bring me a can of green paint. What? Where should you look for it? Here! In the house! Sergeant Lombardo. Find out what the devil Dr. Meléndez is doing. He knows I'm too busy to be waiting around for him all day!"

The three men departed like shots, while two others began to dust all the flat surfaces in the house with different colored fingerprint powders. It wasn't hot but Inspector Jiménez brought his finger up to his collar and loosened his tie with one jerk. "Well, what do you think?" he appealed to Daniel.

"It looks like murder," he said slowly.

"Oh! So it looks like murder, eh?" whined the inspector. "Thank you so very much, *señor* Hernández!"

"I was going to say," Daniel continued calmly, "that it looks like murder—with some interesting twists."

"You've got to find him," cried Altabe urgently. He clenched his powerful fists tightly. *"Give him to me!* Today. Even if he's

186

someone in my own house . . ."

The celebrated athlete stopped suddenly.

"We'll do everything possible," the inspector said slowly. "First we have to find the murderer. Then, the law—"

"The law!" exclaimed Altabe disdainfully, smashing a fist into a meaty palm. He tottered for a moment, wordlessly, then dropped into an armchair, overcome by his own anger. Daniel perceived in the man, a colossus in size, the first signs of age. He was almost bald, and on his forehead a swollen blue vein pulsed rapidly.

"All right," he murmured quietly. "I suppose this is all useless . . . I don't want to delay your investigation. There'll be time . . . afterwards. Oh, yes, there'll be time."

Inspector Jiménez turned away from him to consult his papers. They had removed the corpse, and the police doctor had since passed on a preliminary report to him. *Death by strangulation effected between nine and eleven in the morning.* The autopsy would perhaps permit this period to be cut down somewhat.

There were no other signs of violence in the room. The glass doors enclosed an impressive collection of trophies, medals, and parchments. From the walls hung a multitude of objects linked to Altabe's sports activities: pennants and colors, a baseball glove, a billiard cue and a polo mallet, a little rubber squash ball with the inscription "National Championship—1936—First Place," a squash racquet with a similar legend, and autographed photos of Andrada, Carrera, and naturally Bernabé Ferreyra.

The inspector had quickly abandoned robbery as a motive. There was nothing of value missing in the house. The criminal obviously had entered and left by the street door, because in the fresh earth of the garden and the flower beds bordering it there were no footprints.

The fingerprint men had completed their job. From the beginning it appeared that the only prints to be found were those of the occupants of the house: Mariana, her sister, and Altabe. Two other groups of prints probably belonged to the house servants who, since it was Sunday, had the day off.

"Anything you could suggest might be helpful," said Jiménez, glancing up at Altabe. "The first thing we have to find out, of course, is if your wife had any enemies."

Altabe uttered a brief, sullen laugh.

"Someone hated her enough to kill her. I would never have believed she had an enemy in the world. She was married earlier, but her husband died. My first wife also died."

The inspector grunted comprehension. "Did your wife leave a large estate?"

"I never concerned myself about her finances."

"Oh, I see." Jiménez cleared his throat noisily. "I have to ask you now a rather unpleasant but necessary question. Is it possible, remotely possible shall we say, that the crime could have been motivated by passion?"

Gregorio Altabe's face grew slowly red. He made a move to get up, a homicidal spark showing in his eyes. Then, with equally quick decision he began to laugh.

"Don't be silly," he said simply.

"Very well. That eliminates one of the motives which must always be considered. Can you tell me where *you* were between nine and eleven this morning?"

Altabe lit a cigarette with trembling hand and then regarded the ribbon of smoke closely.

"I see you're not forgetting your business. Well, you're right, of course. Yes, I can tell you. At five minutes past nine I left home and walked to the repair shop where I had my car. I talked with the garage mechanic until quarter to ten. Then I went for a ride. I wanted to try out the car to see if it ran all right. I went as far as San Isidro. And when I returned . . ."

His face grew red again. The inspector interrupted him hastily.

"Did you meet anyone you knew on the road?"

"No."

"Well, I suppose it's not important," lied the inspector. "Routine inquiries. Now, the last question: do you have a can of green paint in the house?"

"Paint? What do you mean?"

188

"Nothing special," said the inspector, smiling. "An idea of mine. But if you don't know anything about it, I think we can let you go now."

"One moment, Inspector," interposed Daniel Hernández. "I'd like to ask a question, if you've no objection."

Jiménez nodded.

"*Señor* Altabe, are you still active in sports?"

The athlete looked at Daniel as if he were seeing him for the first time, although the latter had not been absent from the room during the entire interrogation. He fixed his eyes at some point on the ceiling and responded in a low voice, "Not as much as before. But still, I think—" he gently rubbed his clenched fist in the palm of his other hand—"I think I can kill a man with one blow."

"I wasn't thinking of that," said Daniel firmly. "I was referring to other sports."

"What sports?"

His tone had become unmistakably aggressive.

"Baseball, for example. Or tennis, or—"

Gregorio Altabe sighed. "No," he said sadly. "I'm not as young as I used to be. Those years for me are far, far behind . . ."

The woman impeccably dressed in black was Angélica Lerner, the victim's sister; but there were no traces of tears on her makeup. She was a tall brunette, about thirty-five years old. She gave the address of the friend's house where she had been between ten and eleven that morning. From nine to ten, she declared, she had been taking in the sun at a nearby park. Unfortunately, she had seen no one she knew.

"And what do you know about your sister's death?"

"Nothing. Poor Mariana. I told her—"

She bit her lip, leaving the sentence unfinished. But the inspector's ideas in regard to incomplete sentences were quite well defined.

189

"You told her? You told her what?"

"Nothing. Please excuse me. My nerves are carrying me away."

The inspector made a face. He had never known a single woman in all his experience who didn't prefer to be pressed to reveal what she knew.

"You told your sister that it was going to end this way. Why?"

"I don't know. I must have misspoken."

The inspector was undisturbed. He called Sergeant Lombardo. "Escort this woman to the Palacio de Justicia," he said. "Place her incommunicado—at the disposition of the criminal judge."

He got up, signalling the end of the interview.

The woman turned visibly pale and dropped into an armchair. "All right," she said, smiling vaguely. "You don't think it was *I* who killed Mariana?"

"I don't think. A bad habit. You're the one who has to think."

"Well, I didn't. I have no ideas about anyone else. The fact is we've almost always lived apart. But during the short time I've been here, I've come to love her more than ever before. Although—at times I criticized her—her conduct."

"What do you mean?"

"Men. Do I have to go into detail?"

"That would be preferable. What men?"

"Oh, anyone. Poor Mariana never established many preferences. I never criticized her for moral scruples, understand that. But I always advised moderation. She paid no attention . . . And this is the result."

"Can you identify any of the men?"

"I can tell you of no one specifically."

The inspector exchanged glances with Daniel.

"Did the husband know?"

"Who, Gregorio?" She shrugged her shoulders. "I doubt it."

"Your sister was married once before?"

"Yes. The first husband was a wealthy businessman. It was from him that she inherited the fortune." She paused. "Now it passes into Gregorio's hands. Compulsory inheritance."

190

"And you?"

"I don't know if there are any legacies in Mariana's will or not."

"Are you sure your sister left a will?" injected Daniel.

She looked at him intensely. She didn't seem convinced of the need to answer, but a gesture from the inspector decided her.

"I don't know," she replied. "Probably not. She wasn't thinking about dying."

"Any insurance?" persisted Daniel.

"Yes. I was going to mention it. A hundred and fifty thousand *pesos*—in my name."

"Her idea?"

"No, mine. I've always been afraid of being left destitute. On Mariana's part it was a generous impulse, I suppose. A way of telling me she was happy to have me here—at her side."

"You don't think much of your sister's husband," ventured the inspector.

"I don't have anything against Gregorio," she replied, measuring her words carefully. "I knew he was a famous athlete, champion in a lot of things . . . years ago, of course. I suppose it was that aura of sporting glory that attracted Mariana. At least . . ."

"At least for a while?" said the inspector, completing the sentence for her.

"That wasn't what I meant."

At this moment, the face of Sergeant Lombardo appeared at the door and signalled with a questioning look.

"Have him come in," ordered the inspector. "But before you do, call the laboratory and see what the results are."

"May I go?" asked the woman.

"Yes," said the inspector. "Thank you for your cooperation."

If there was any irony in the formality, Angélica Lerner showed no sign of being aware of it. Coolly excusing herself, she left.

"Well, what do you think?" asked Jiménez. "And don't tell me it looks like murder!"

"It's exactly what it seems," replied Daniel kindly. "A murder

191

plus some partial alibis. I'm inclined to think that that woman is uncommonly interested in seeing the guilt pinned on her brother-in-law."

"Why?"

"Oh, come now, it's very simple. If Altabe were the murderer, he couldn't inherit the fortune, of course. *Ergo* . . ."

"So you think she's guilty?"

Daniel smiled. "Really now," he said. "You can't be serious. I haven't the slightest idea."

"Common paint, inspector," announced Lombardo, sticking his head through the doorway again. "For painting doors and windows. A high quality paint, imported. Nothing unusual about it."

"Order a complete analysis. And if you see Ramírez, get him in here."

As Lombardo disappeared from the doorway, Ramírez, the detective who had gone off in search of the paint, entered hurriedly with a can in his hand.

"Here it is, sir."

"Ah, yes. Leave it here."

"It wasn't in the house, sir. It was in the place next door. I think we've found the murderer."

The inspector jumped up. "Who?"

"Esteban Valverde is his name, sir. A neighbor of ours," he explained. "That is, I mean, a neighbor of these people."

"Are you sure?" Jiménez demanded. "This isn't a lot of nonsense, now?"

"Positive," replied the detective.

He appeared to be still an adolescent; and he was afraid. Fear glazed his large, dark eyes, half-opened mouth, and vibrated through the long-fingered hands. The bustle of the crowd of men hardly altered his immobility; it shook him imperceptibly, like a leaf.

"Is it really true?" he asked in a low, almost inaudible voice.

No one answered him.

"She's dead," he said. "It's true, then, that she's dead." The boy seemed to be on the point of tears. "I'm the guilty one," he murmured. "I killed her."

The inspector felt a shock in the pit of his stomach. He sat the boy down and put a hand on his shoulder. "What was it all about, son?"

Esteban flinched at the inspector's touch as if he had been struck. He gazed down at his long, strong fingers. It seemed as though he were seeing them for the first time. "What do you mean?" he said. "I don't know what you mean."

The inspector exhaled noisily. "Very well, let's start over again. Didn't you just say that you killed her?"

The youth looked back with anger, almost with repugnance. "Me? *Mariana?*" He scrutinized the men who surrounded him, as if the world had suddenly gone mad and he was seeking somewhere a trace of sanity. "What are you saying?"

"The inspector thinks that you killed *señora* Altabe," said Daniel smoothly. "You yourself just said—"

Esteban ran his hand through his hair in a disoriented gesture.

"Oh, yes. I did say that. Now I understand . . ." He smiled confusedly, but the fear in his eyes remained. "I meant to say something else. I meant to say that if I—"

The inspector came down to earth with a sudden change of tone. In a thundering voice he exclaimed, "Just a minute. Let's get this straight right now. You killed *señora* Altabe. Yes or no?"

He had lost his paternal attitude.

"No. I didn't kill her."

Jiménez turned and strode like a fury to where Ramírez was standing. The latter looked as if he'd like to cut a hole in the floor and drop through.

"Well, what have you got to say now?"

"Don't pay any attention to him, Inspector. He swears he didn't know, Inspector. But he was the one for sure, believe me. Let's have a look, Junior," he exclaimed, trying to capture a little mastery over the embarrassing situation. "Show the inspector your hands."

193

Esteban didn't move. Jiménez stalked over to the suspect and roughly raised the boy's hands. The index finger of the right hand had several dry green paint stains on it. And on the back of his left hand was another green paint smear.

A slow smile came over the inspector's face.

"All right," he said. "You don't have to say anything more. Those stains speak for themselves. Deny it all you want!"

Daniel's petulant voice shook the inspector's poise.

"Excuse me, Inspector," he murmured, "but it would seem to me that, to put it one way, paint-stained hands aren't necessarily the same as blood-stained hands."

"What the devil—"

"Just that it's possible that this lad can explain how he got paint stains on his hands."

"Oh, you think so, eh? Then perhaps he can explain how he happened to paint the neck and dress of the corpse, too!"

Esteban appeared detached from what was occurring about him.

"Now look here," Jiménez persisted. "You—you get busy explaining this or I'll pack you off somewhere where you can think it over for a while!"

The boy went pale again. His hands continued to tremble. "All right," he said weakly. "What do you want me to explain?"

"Everything. *Every—thing.* Why did you say you killed her?"

"I meant it was my fault. She wanted us to run away together. I was afraid to. I knew that my father would have died for shame."

The inspector looked at him with absolute incredulity.

"You—you were her lover?" he stammered.

Esteban blushed deeply.

"You don't have to talk that way," he said. "You don't have to—"

"I'll talk as I please," the officer cut in, now furious. "Where are your parents?"

"They're not at home. They're spending the weekend out of the city."

"Why are you smeared with paint?"

194

"I was painting some shutters."

"Ah, some shutters! How nice! Nothing more than shutters?"

"I don't know what you mean."

"Show me the shutters."

Esteban got up and opened the glass casement window that faced onto the patio. At the left of the patio, in a wing of the same building, were two windows: one on the ground floor, opening from a bedroom, and another higher up that seemed to face out from a garret. The shutter on the garret window was entirely of wood and had recently been painted green. There was a tall ladder leaning against the wall, and at the foot of it a newspaper, a paint brush, a metal scraping brush, and a can of turpentine. It was there that Ramírez had found the can of paint.

At the right of the patio a six-foot-high wall divided the property from the garden of the home next door where the murder had taken place. A part of the house and an edge of the garden could be seen over the top of the wall.

The inspector went outside and examined every nook and cranny of the patio, which was laid with white paving stones decorated with pale blue designs, without discovering anything of note.

Turning about he discovered Daniel Hernández perched at the top of the ladder making strange gestures, like a trained monkey, in front of the solid wood garret shutter.

"What are you up to now?" he shouted. "It's a painted shutter, that's all!"

Daniel inched down with extravagant care, brushed his hands off on his coat and smiled happily.

"I know it," he replied. "I wanted to know if it was also an unpainted shutter."

The inspector shrugged his shoulders unappreciatively. He was seldom in the mood for jokes.

*   *   *

Esteban Valverde's room, where the final questioning was taking place, was a sort of library, with solid antique furniture.

On top of the old, low desk there was a vast mass of disorganized papers. The inspector looked them over with repugnance.

"All right, Valverde," he opened in a cool, measured tone, "what did you do this morning?"

"I was painting that shutter and—"

"Yes, I know," interrupted the inspector. "Afterwards."

"From nine o'clock to ten I listened to a concert. The state broadcast. Works of Mozart."

"Note that," the inspector said, turning to Lombardo. "What else?"

"From ten o'clock on I was writing."

"What were you writing?"

Esteban blinked nervously but did not answer.

"What were you writing?" demanded Jiménez.

"Poetry," mumbled the boy.

The inspector broke into rude laughter.

"Ah, poetry! I should have known. May we see your verse?"

Esteban made a quick movement towards the desk. Ramírez and Carletti followed, but the inspector beat them all and emerged triumphantly, waving above a jumble of arms a single sheet of manuscript. Only the first two lines of the poem were perfectly legible, written in the precise hand of a student. The rest was a confusion of erasures, unfinished lines, fragmentary metrical schemes that illusorily finished them, and probable rhymes in vertical columns. The two initial lines were hendecasyllables:

> *In the shadow of a bird that passes by*
> *Darting time I see on silent wings to fly . . .*

The inspector snorted contemptuously.

"What were you going to put after 'fly'?" he grunted. "Sigh?"

He handed the sheet over to Daniel who read the lines with profound attention. In the middle of his reading, a striking change suddenly came over him: the vertical furrow of his forehead deepened; his eyes, absorbed in thought, seemed to be turning in on a secret region of his soul. Quickly he turned on

Esteban. "What gave you the idea for this poem?" he asked with more asperity than was common for him.

"Oh," replied the boy slowly, "time . . . change . . . the brevity of it all—"

"Yes, yes, I know," interrupted Daniel impatiently. "I wasn't talking about that. Something else. Ideas don't just come out of the blue. Something fires them and gives them life. Something which could be insignificant, but which is now decisive. Think! Try to remember!"

Esteban stroked his head thoughtfully. Twice he shook it, discouraged. Then, suddenly he raised his eyes towards Daniel in great astonishment.

"Now I know," he said. "But how—how did you—"

"*What was it?*" insisted Daniel.

"A bird," he answered. "Now I remember. I wouldn't have dreamed—"

Jiménez clamped his hands to his head. "Oh, no, no, no, no!" he cried with the precision of a machine-gun. "Not this! Don't give me any business about birds now! This is *mur-der!*"

"Shhhh," urged Daniel, turning back to the boy. "You saw it? And I mean *saw it?*"

"No. I saw the shadow. Now I understand what gave me the idea for the first lines. That's why I wrote them so quickly. But I don't see—"

"Never mind," interrupted Daniel. "You saw a bird's shadow. You saw it pass in the patio, isn't that right?"

"Yes, I had sat down to write. Nothing came to my mind. I looked outside. The white paving stones were brilliant in the sunlight. The shadow crossed the patio—like an arrow—then returned instantly."

"It came from the right?"

"Yes."

"And you had the doors closed. You saw it through the glass panels, didn't you?"

"Yes, but how—"

"One last question. Think carefully. *What time was it?*"

197

"That's easy," replied Esteban. "The concert ended at ten. It lasted an hour. So it must have been about five minutes after ten."

Daniel Hernández released a pent-up sigh of relief and turned a pensive smile to Inspector Jiménez. "A bird passes," he murmured. "Even less than that—the shadow of a bird—and a poem is born. Tell me, Inspector, is there anything more trifling, more insubstantial, more immaterial than the shadow of a bird? There's a mystery for you that's greater than the one you're now investigating."

"That's all very nice," said the inspector. "But that's not a solution."

"Yes. Very nice," agreed Daniel, pointing out the window. "But that wasn't a bird!"

"Ugh!" snorted the inspector. "That was a bad moment—when you went back and faced Altabe, and told him he had killed his wife. If we'd let him, he'd have killed you!" He ran his hand along his right cheek bone where a bruise attested to the potency of the old champion's fist.

"Your boys are very efficient," said Daniel smiling. "I never dreamed that Ramírez knew judo."

"Oh, I do too," Jiménez commented modestly.

They were walking along a street in the quiet Belgrano residential district, flanked by trees, peaceful in the half-shade of dusk.

"How you figured Altabe got to that paint I can't imagine," said Jiménez. "The can was in the house next door. Altabe couldn't have jumped the wall without leaving footprints in his own garden. And he couldn't have entered the house by the street door and crossed the patio without Valverde seeing him."

"It's very simple," said Daniel. "He used a squash ball."

"*A squash ball?*"

"A rubber ball."

"Then that was—"

"Yes, that was the shadow that Esteban saw streaking across

the patio of his home. The shadow of a bird. A rubber bird, fleeting and well-aimed, which crosses in a second and returns instantly—"

The inspector looked at him questioningly.

"Can we prove it?"

"Of course. Almost in the very center of the garret shutter is a little circular impression, about an inch to an inch and a half across. The unmistakable impression of a ball. Esteban saw the shadow pass a few minutes after ten. Of the two occupants of the house next door, Gregorio Altabe is the only one who has no alibi for that time."

"You suspected him, then, when you climbed down the ladder."

"Yes. When I saw the shutter I remembered the trophy room. Every sport that Altabe played implied mastery in the manipulation of a ball. And the person who launched that ball so it would bounce off a shutter situated some thirty feet away, and hit the mark almost in the exact center, certainly possessed that skill.

"Altabe knew about what was going on between Mariana and Esteban. Eliminating his wife, then, he was killing two birds with one stone: he was satisfying his desire for revenge and was ending up with a fortune to boot. And if along the way he could incriminate Valverde and have him shipped off to prison, then the plan was perfect. Esteban himself presented Altabe with the opportunity when he began painting the garret shutters which faced Altabe's own place. The murderer waited for him to finish, sent the ball flying with great force and deadly accuracy against the painted wood surface, caught it on the fly and set about to take care of her."

"The quantity of paint that can adhere to a squash ball isn't great, but for Altabe it was sufficient to leave on the neck and clothing of the body markings that were destined to implicate Valverde. You'll remember that you yourself had difficulty in perceiving the paint traces on the victim's throat. I had thought it was just a print in the material too."

Inspector Jiménez nodded, quite satisfied.

"The murderer," Daniel continued, "didn't use a very big ball, one that would lose its force on hitting against a sticky surface. I rather think it was one of those extraordinarily resilient balls that you've often seen bounding with enormous speed and force off the walls of a squash court.

"Any other person less expert than he would have thrown the ball. Altabe, I think, drove it with a squash racquet. Perhaps the same one with which he won the National Championship in 1936 . . ."

CHECKMATE IN TWO MOVES
W. I. Eisen

*W. I. Eisen is the pseudonym of Isaac Aisemberg, an Argentine TV and film writer who, some twenty years ago, produced two of the best detective novels ever written in the Spanish language —*Three Negatives for One Photo *(1949) and* Blood in the Bermejo River *(1950). He has written only a few detective short stories, but of these "Checkmate in Two Moves" is a fine example of what he does best. The exterior setting is Buenos Aires, but the real focus of the narrative is the mind of a man who has poisoned his uncle and is calmly (really not so calmly) carrying through the steps of a carefully calculated murder plan. The reader knows the plot must fail at some point, but does not learn how until the last words of the story. Then, suddenly it is all clear. The plan* hasn't *failed, but yet the murderer is caught. But actually, he's not caught. Or maybe he is . . . "Checkmate in Two Moves" is, no matter what the reader may conclude, a neatly fashioned tale of irony.*

Checkmate in Two Moves

W. I. E I S E N

YES, I poisoned him. It turned out well, and I am not in the least remorseful. And now in two hours I shall be a free man and my own master. It was ten in the evening when I left Uncle Nestor with a feeling of unrestrained triumph, and set out on a serene walk down the avenue in the general direction of the waterfront.

I felt buoyant and unburdened, and it amused me to reflect that even Guillermo was profiting by the deal. Poor Guillermo! He was so timid, so reticent that I had known from the first I would have to act for both of us. I had foreseen the necessity on the day when we had been taken as orphans into a home as palatial as it was cold—a home where affection did not exist. It was as predetermined and as certain as the constant, daily click of coins around us.

"You've got to get into the habit of not squandering," Uncle Nestor would proclaim. "Don't forget, my entire fortune will be yours one day."

We would look at each other, Guillermo and I, and we would smile. But unfortunately the arrival of that wonderful day seemed constantly to recede despite the fact that Uncle had serious gall bladder attacks and was, in addition, suffering from heart trouble.

As far as his domineering attitude was concerned it went steadily from bad to worse, becoming well-nigh intolerable when Guillermo had the ill-grace to fall in love. Uncle Nestor just didn't like the girl.

"She comes from an impoverished family," he cold-bloodedly pointed out. "She lacks refinement. She's a *nobody*."

203

Guillermo accomplished nothing by enumerating the young lady's good points. The old man was as pig-headedly stubborn as he was unpredictable.

With me, however, he was far more circumspect, for I presented him with a more disturbing problem—a conflict of personalities. He had set his mind on my acquiring a doctorate in chemistry at the university. But the investment had proven a poor one, and he found himself the uncle of a card sharp and horse-racing expert instead. Naturally, he did not contribute in any way to these diverting pastimes of mine. And it took some real ingenuity on my part to pry him loose from a single *peso*.

One of my favorite deceptive practices was to endure without complaint his interminable chess games. When I was beaten, I would give in with good humor and a smile. But, on the other hand, when he was in a favorable position he would lengthen out the game painfully, analyzing each move with revolting deliberation, aware of my desire to hurry off to the club. He savored my torment with a sadistic satisfaction as he sipped his cognac.

One day he said to me with insulting irony: "It gratifies me to see that you've studiously applied yourself to the game. You are connivingly intelligent and an infamous loafer. But nevertheless your devotion shall have its reward. I'm quite fair, you see. From now on—since you're not getting a diploma—I'll keep track of our chess matches. How does that sound to you, lad? I'll copy the scores in a notebook, and keep a day-to-day record of our debts."

I realized then that if I bowed to his tyranny, I could clear several hundred *pesos* a week. So I accepted. From that moment on I became a slave to statistics. So absorbed was he in the outcome of his gamble that in my absence he fell into the habit of playing solitaire chess, with himself, and even discussed the matches with Julio, the butler.

Well, it is all a receding nightmare now. I had dared greatly and I had found a way out. It could hardly have been called a pleasant way. But is death by violence ever pleasant?

204

I was approaching Costanera now. It was a wet, sultry night, and across the clouded sky darted flashes of heat lightning. The humidity dampened my hands and parched my mouth. At the corner an approaching policeman made my heart leap. Then he passed and I breathed again.

The poison—what was it called? Aconite. I had slipped it secretly out of the laboratory at school, and had deposited a few drops in his cognac surreptitiously. Uncle had been charming for once. Graciously he had excused me from the game.

"I'll make it a solitaire," he said. "I gave the servants the evening off. It may seem strange to you, but tonight I want to be alone. Afterwards I'll read a good book. A man is wise when he surrenders completely to his mood of the moment. Go ahead."

"Thank you, Uncle," I said. "I would not have suggested it ordinarily. But today *is* Saturday, and—"

The devil! How well did he understand? Was it the clairvoyance of a condemned man? But I was sure I could carry it off.

But what of Guillermo? Undoubtedly Guillermo was a problem. I had met him in the hall immediately following my "carelessness" with the aconite. He was coming down the stairs, looking very preoccupied.

"What's the matter?" I asked him cheerfully, and I would have gladly added: "*Ah, if you only knew!*"

"I'm fed up," he replied. "I've had about as much of him as I can stand!"

"Come on!" I said, slapping him on the back. "Whatever it is —it won't seem half so bad tomorrow."

"It's bound to seem worse," he muttered. "He's driving me crazy. Between him and Mathilde—"

"What about Mathilde?"

"She gave me an ultimatum. I must choose between her and Uncle."

"Choose her," I said quickly. "It's what I'd do."

He looked at me with a despairing gleam in his eyes. Without my encouragement the poor fellow would never have made the slightest move to resolve his difficulties.

205

"That's what I'd do too," he said quickly. "But what would we live on? You know how merciless he is. He'd deprive me of everything."

"Well, perhaps if we're patient things will take care of themselves," I said. "Who knows . . ."

Guillermo's lips tightened. He shook his head. "There's no way out. I'm trapped. But I'm going to have a talk with him. Where is he now?"

I was frightened, knowing that if the poison had worked slowly, and if the first symptoms had not brought on convulsions, he could still be helped and—a coldness crept up my spine.

"He's in the library," I said. "But leave him alone. When he finished the chess game he dismissed the servants. The old fool would be furious if you broke in on him now. He wants to be alone. Go forget your troubles at a bar."

He thought a few moments and when at last he spoke he seemed relieved. "I'll see him some other time then. After all—"

"After all, you wouldn't want to get upset," I said severely.

Guillermo fixed his gaze on me. For a moment he seemed angry, but the mood passed almost instantly.

I looked at my watch. "It's nearly eleven now," I said, aloud to myself.

No doubt it had begun by this time. First there'd be a slight sense of discomfort in the pit of his stomach. Then a sharp little pain, but nothing very alarming. He'd probably start cursing the cook.

Now, with the thought of it sharp in my mind, my calmness amazed me a little. The paving stones were distorted into rhombs, and the river was a dirty stain along the thick wall. In the distance I could see lights—green, red, and white. The automobiles moved swiftly along, their tires skimming the asphalt.

I walked on for ten more minutes, and then decided that I had gone far enough, and that it would be safe to return.

*   *   *

Once again I was on the avenue heading for Leandro N. Alem. From there to the Plaza de Mayo was only a few steps. My watch returned me to reality. The hour hand pointed to 11:30. If the poison had worked quickly, I would have nothing further to fear. Uncle would have suffered a simple heart attack and I—would be his very fortunate heir.

I entered a bar. A juke box was playing a popular melody and the waiter seemed surprised by my grim expression, and my undoubted pallor.

"Sir," he said. "Is there anything wrong?"

"I'm quite all right," I assured him. "Bring me a cognac."

"Very well, sir," he said. "You must forgive me. I—well, for a moment I thought you might have had an attack."

Through the windows I watched the passing caravan, the imagined ticks of my watch dominating every other sound in the place, even the beating of my heart. One o'clock came and went. I drank the cognac in a single gulp.

At 2:30 I returned home. At first I suspected nothing—not until someone stepped out to block my path. In the dim light I could just make out the figure of a policeman, and a sudden, terrible fear possessed me.

"*Señor* Claudio Alvarez?" he asked.

I nodded.

"Come in," the policeman said, stepping away from the doorway.

"W-what are you doing here?" I stammered.

"You'll know quickly enough," was his slow, dry reply.

In the hall I saw several uniformed men who appeared to have taken possession of the house. Julio, the butler, tried to talk to me. But the officer in charge, a gray-haired man with flashing dark eyes, silenced him with a gesture. The officer immediately turned, and stared at me coldly.

"Are you one of the two nephews?" he asked.

"Yes, sir," I murmured. "The eldest. My brother—"

"I'm sorry to tell you that your uncle has been murdered," he said. "I am Inspector Villegas, in charge of the investigation. I must ask you to accompany me to the next room."

207

I followed him into the library. Two assistants fell in behind us. Inspector Villegas gestured towards a chair and seated himself at the desk. He lit a cigarette, and continued to eye me coldly.

"You are the nephew Claudio?" He spoke as if he were repeating a lesson he had committed to memory, and could ill-afford not to get it right.

"Yes, sir," I said.

"Well, then, explain what you did last night."

"The three of us had dinner together as usual," I said, choosing my words with care. "Guillermo retired to his room. Uncle and I remained to chat for awhile and then, at his suggestion, we went to the library. After we finished our customary game of chess I said goodnight and left. In the vestibule I ran into Guillermo who had come downstairs, and was just going out. We exchanged a few words, and then—I left alone."

"And now you're returning?"

"Yes," I said.

"What about the servants?"

"Uncle let them go after dinner—insisted on their going, in fact. He wanted to be completely alone in the house. From time to time he'd do strange things like that."

"Your account agrees for the most part with what the butler has told us. When he returned he made his customary routine check upstairs and down. He noticed that the library door was partly open and that light was shining out. When he entered the room he found your uncle seated before the chess game, dead. The game had been interrupted. So you were engaging in a little gambling match with him tonight, eh?"

For a moment I couldn't seem to breathe. My mouth was dry, and my heart had begun a furious pounding. *Uncle's well-known solitary games!*

"Yes, sir," I admitted, my voice almost failing me.

The inspector had probably already dragged Guillermo over the same coals. Where *was* Guillermo? Was it the inspector's plan to isolate us, to leave us alone, defenseless, and then to pick us apart?

208

"You were apparently in the habit of making a written record of your games with your uncle—to keep the details straight. Will you please show me that record book, *señor* Alvarez?"

I was sinking into a mire. "Record book?" I asked.

"Certainly, my good fellow. My wanting to see it should not surprise you. A police officer must verify everything. Before I leave this house I must satisfy myself that *you played the same as always.*"

I began to stutter. "Well, the truth is . . ." And then, in an outburst I couldn't control, "Of course we played the same as always!"

Tears began to sting my eyes. They had me—they had me! They were deliberately, maliciously playing with my desperation. They were amusing themselves with my guilt.

Suddenly the inspector asid, accusingly: "You were the last one to see him alive. And also—the first to see him dead. Your uncle made no notation in the book this time, my good friend!"

I don't know why I stood up, tense, despairing. "All right!" I cried. "If you know, why ask me? I killed him because I hated him with all my soul. I could no longer stand his tyranny."

The inspector seemed genuinely startled. "Good heavens," he said. "He gave in sooner than I had hoped. All right," he said, turning on me, "since you've decided to confess, where's the revolver?"

"Wh-what revolver?" I stammered.

Inspector Villegas didn't lose his calm. He replied imperturbably, "Come on, don't pretend your memory needs to be refreshed. The revolver! Or have you forgotten that you murdered him with one shot. One shot square between the eyes. Lord, what superb marksmanship!"

DEATH AND THE COMPASS
Jorge Luis Borges

The last story of this collection is, in the editor's opinion, the most extraordinary detective story ever written in Spanish America. Jorge Luis Borges' "Death and the Compass" was published in 1942, the same year in which the volume of Six Problems for don Isidro Parodi *appeared under the Borges-Bioy pen name of H. Bustos Domecq. It is one of the stories included in* Ficciones *(1944), Borges' finest collection of original prose tales, all of which save two were written after 1938, the year in which Borges nearly died from septicemia. Fearing that the seventeen days of fever, delirium and hallucination he had suffered before his recovery had affected his "mental integrity," he determined to try something at which he had not proven his ability—the composition of short stories. If he had tried to write a critical essay or a poem and had failed, he felt he would have proof of the deterioration of his mind. But by trying something different, he could attribute an unsuccessful result to the natural consequences of inexperience. (We need say nothing of the "integrity" of an intellect that was capable of conceiving this argument.) The stories Borges now began to write found their way into* Ficciones *and later into a volume of subsequent narratives collected under the title* The Aleph *(1949). It is mainly on the merits of these two volumes that Borges today figures as a prominent candidate for the Nobel Prize for Literature. In "Death and the Compass" Borges blends his fondness for the detective story together with a view of a "nightmare version of Buenos Aires" into a story wherein poetry, fantasy and metaphysics permeate and transform the fixed detective story pattern. Repeated readings of this masterly store will not exhaust its melancholy beauty and fascination.*

Death and the Compass
JORGE LUIS BORGES

OF the many problems which exercised the reckless discernment
of Lönnrot, none was so strange—so rigorously strange, shall
we say—as the periodically spaced series of bloody events which
culminated at the villa of Triste-le-Roy, amid the ceaseless
aroma of the eucalypti. It is true that Erik Lönnrot failed to
prevent the last murder, but that he foresaw it is indisputable.
Again, he did not guess the identity of Yarmolinsky's luckless
assassin, but he did succeed in divining the secret plan behind
the fiendish series, as well as the participation of Red Scharlach,
whose other nickname is Scharlach the Dandy. That criminal
(like countless others) had sworn on his honor to kill Lönnrot,
but the latter could never be intimidated. Lönnrot believed himself a pure reasoner, an Auguste Dupin; but there was something of the adventurer in him, even a little of the gambler.

The first murder occurred in the Hotel du Nord, that tall
prism which dominates the estuary whose waters are the color
of sand. To that tower (which quite glaringly unites the hateful
whiteness of a sanatorium, the numbered divisibility of a jail, and
the general appearance of a bordello) there came, on the third
day of December, the delegate from Podolsk to the Third
Talmudic Congress, Dr. Marcel Yarmolinsky, a gray-bearded
man with gray eyes. We shall never know whether the Hotel du
Nord pleased him; he accepted it with the ancient resignation
which had allowed him to endure three years of war in the
Carpathians and three thousand years of oppression and
pogroms. He was given a room on floor R, across from the suite
which was occupied—not without splendor—by the Tetrarch of
Galilee. Yarmolinsky supped, postponed until the following day

213

an inspection of the unknown city, arranged on a shelf his many books and few personal possessions, and before midnight extinguished his light. (Thus declared the Tetrarch's chauffeur, who slept in the adjoining room.) On the fourth, at 11:30 A.M., the editor of the *Yiddishe Zeitung* put in a call to him; Dr. Yarmolinsky did not answer. He was found in his room, his face already a little dark, nearly nude beneath a large, archaic cape. He was lying not far from the door, which opened on the hall; a deep knife wound had split his breast. A few hours later, in the same room, amid journalists, photographers, and policemen, Inspector Treviranus and Lönnrot were calmly discussing the problem.

"No need to look for a three-legged cat here," Treviranus was saying, as he brandished an imperious cigar. "We all know that the Tetrarch of Galilee owns the finest sapphires in the world. Someone, intending to steal them, must have broken in here by mistake. Yarmolinsky got up; the robber had to kill him. How does it sound to you?"

"Possible, but not interesting," Lönnrot answered. "You'll reply that reality hasn't the least obligation to be interesting. And I'll answer you that reality may avoid that obligation, but that hypotheses may not. In the hypothesis that you propose, chance intervenes heavily. Here we have a dead rabbi: I would prefer a purely rabbinical explanation, not the imaginary mischances of an imaginary robber."

Treviranus replied ill-humoredly, "I'm not interested in rabbinical explanations. I am interested in capturing the man who stabbed this unknown person."

"Not so unknown," corrected Lönnrot. "Here are his complete works." He indicated on the shelf a row of tall books: a *Vindication of the Cabala, An Explanation of the Philosophy of Robert Fludd,* a literal translation of the *Sepher Yezirah,* a *Biography of the Baal Shem,* a *History of the Hasidim,* a monograph (in German) on the Tetragrammaton, another on the divine nomenclature of the Pentateuch.

The Inspector regarded them with dread, almost with repulsion. Then he began to laugh. "I'm a poor Christian," he said.

214

"Carry off those musty volumes if you want; I don't have any time to lose in Jewish superstitions."

"Maybe the crime belongs to the history of Jewish superstitions," murmured Lönnrot.

"Like Christianity," the editor of the *Yiddishe Zeitung* ventured to add. He was myopic, an atheist, and very shy.

No one answered him. One of the agents had found a piece of paper in the small typewriter, on which was written the following unfinished sentence: *The first letter of the Name has been uttered.*

Lönnrot abstained from smiling. Suddenly become a bibliophile or Hebraist, he ordered a package made of the dead man's books and carried them off to his apartment. Indifferent to the police investigation, he dedicated himself to studying the books. One large octavo volume revealed to him the teachings of Israel Baal Shem Tobh, founder of the sect of the Pious; another, the virtues and terrors of the Tetragrammaton, which is the unutterable name of God; another, the thesis that God has a secret name, in which is epitomized (as in the crystal sphere which the Persians ascribe to Alexander of Macedonia) his ninth attribute, eternity—that is to say, the immediate knowledge of all things that will be, which are, and which have been in the universe. Tradition numbers ninety-nine names of God; the Hebrews attribute that imperfect number to the magic fears of even numbers; the Hasidim reason that that hiatus indicates a hundredth name—the Absolute Name.

From this erudition Lönnrot was distracted, a few days later, by the appearance of the editor of the *Yiddishe Zeitung*. The latter wanted to talk about the murder; Lönnrot preferred to discuss the diverse names of God; the journalist declared, in three columns, that the investigator, Erik Lönnrot, had dedicated himself to studying the names of God in order to come across the name of the murderer. Lönnrot, accustomed to the simplifications of journalism, did not become indignant. One of those enterprising shopkeepers, who have discovered that certain books are inevitably bought by certain people, put out a popular edition of the *History of the Sect of Hasidim*.

215

The second murder occurred on the evening of the third of January, in the most deserted and empty corner of the capital's western suburbs. Towards dawn, one of the gendarmes, who patrol those lonely places on horseback, spied a man in a poncho, lying supine in the shadow of an ancient paint shop. The harsh features seemed to be masked in blood; a deep knife wound had split his breast. On the wall, across the yellow, red and green rhombs were some words written in chalk. The gendarme spelled them out ...

That afternoon, Treviranus and Lönnrot headed for the remote scene of the crime. To the left and right of the automobile, the city disintegrated; the firmament grew and houses were of less importance than a brick kiln or a poplar tree. They arrived at their miserable destination: an alley's end, with rose-colored walls which somehow seemed to reflect the diffusive sunset. The dead man had alreay been identified. He was Simon Azevedo, an individual of some fame in the northern suburbs, who had risen from wagon driver to political tough, then degenerated to thief and even informer. (The singular style of his death seemed appropriate to them: Azevedo was the last representative of a generation of bandits who knew how to manipulate a dagger, but not a revolver.) The words in chalk were the following: *The second letter of the Name has been uttered.*

The third murder occurred on the night of the third of February. A little before one o'clock, the telephone in Inspector Treviranus's office rang. In avid secretiveness, a man with a guttural voice spoke; he said his name was Ginzberg (or Ginsburg) and that he was prepared to communicate, for reasonable remuneration, the events surrounding the two sacrifices of Azevedo and Yarmolinsky. A discordant sound of whistles and horns drowned out the informer's voice. Then, the connection was broken off. Without rejecting the possibility of a hoax (after all, it was carnival time), Treviranus found out that he had been called from the Liverpool House, a tavern on the Rue de Toulon, that dingy street where side by side exist the cosmorama and the milk store, the bawdy house and the Bible sellers. Treviranus spoke by phone with the owner. The latter (Black Finnegan, an old Irish criminal, who was immersed in, overcome almost by, respectability) told him that the last person to use the phone was a lodger, a certain Gryphius, who had just left with some friends. Treviranus went immediately to Liverpool House. The owner related to him the following.

Eight days before Gryphius had rented a room above the tavern. He was a sharp-featured man with a nebulous gray beard, and was shabbily dressed in black; Finnegan (who used the room for a purpose which Treviranus guessed) demanded a rent which was undoubtedly excessive; Gryphius paid the stipulated sum without hesitation. He almost never went out; he dined and lunched in his room; his face was scarcely known in the bar. On the night in question, he came downstairs to make a phone call from Finnegan's office. A closed coupé stopped in front of the tavern. The driver didn't move from his seat; several patrons recalled that he was wearing a bear's mask. Two harlequins got out of the coupé; they were of short stature and no one failed to observe that they were very drunk. With a tooting of horns, they burst into Finnegan's office; they embraced Gryphius, who appeared to recognize them, but responded coldly; they exchanged a few words in Yiddish—he in a low, guttural voice; they in high falsetto tones—and then went up to the room. Within a quarter hour the three descended, very happy. Gryphius, staggering, seemed as drunk as the others. He walked—tall and dizzy—in the middle, between the masked harlequins. (One of the women at the bar remembered the yellow, red, and green rhombs.) Twice Gryphius stumbled; twice he was caught and held by the harlequins. Moving off towards the inner harbor, which enclosed a rectangular body of water, the three got into the coupé and disappeared. From the running board of the car, the last of the harlequins scrawled an obscene figure and a sentence on one of the slates of the pier shed.

Treviranus viewed the sentence. It was virtually predictable. It said: *The last of the letters of the Name has been uttered.*

Afterwards, the Inspector examined the small room of Gryphius Ginzberg. On the floor there was a crude star of blood; in the corners, traces of cigarettes of Hungarian manufacture; in a

217

cabinet, a book in Latin, the *Philiogus Hebraeo-Graecus* (1739) of Leusden, with several manuscript notes. Treviranus looked it over with indignation, and had Lönnrot located. The latter, without removing his hat, began to read while the Inspector was interrogating the contradictory witnesses to the possible kidnapping. At four o'clock they left. Out on the twisting Rue de Toulon, where they trod on the dead serpentines of the dawn, Treviranus said, "And what if all this business tonight were just a mock rehearsal?"

Erik Lönnrot smiled and, with all gravity, read a passage (which was underlined) from the thirty-third dissertation of the *Philologus:*

> *Dies Judaeorum incipit a solis occasu*
> *Usque ad solis occasum diei sequentis*

"This means," he added, " 'The Hebrew day begins at sundown and lasts until the following sundown.' "

The Inspector attempted an irony. "Is that fact the most valuable one you've come across tonight?"

"No. Even more valuable was a word that Ginzberg used."

The afternoon papers did not overlook the periodic disappearances. *La Cruz de la Espada* contrasted them with the admirable discipline and order of the last Eremitical Congress; Erns Palast, in *El Mártir,* criticized "the intolerable delays in this clandestine and frugal pogrom, which has taken three months to murder three Jews"; the *Yiddishe Zeitung* rejected the horrible hypothesis of an anti-Semitic plot, "even though many penetrating intellects admit no other solution to the triple mystery"; the most illustrious gunman of the south, Dandy Red Scharlach, swore that in his district similar crimes could never occur, and he accused Inspector Franz Treviranus of criminal negligence.

On the night of March first, the Inspector received an impressive-looking sealed envelope. He opened it; the envelope contained a letter signed Baroj Spinoza and a detailed plan of the city, obviously torn from a Baedeker. The letter prophesied that on the third of March there would not be a fourth murder, since the paint shop in the west, the tavern on the Rue de Toulon, and

218

the Hotel du Nord were "the perfect vertices of a mystic equilateral triangle"; the regularity of the triangle was shown in red ink on the map. Treviranus read the *more geometrico* argument with resignation, and sent the letter and the map to Lönnrot, who, unquestionably, was deserving of such a piece of madness.

Erik Lönnrot studied them. The true locations were, in fact, equidistant. Symmetry in time (the third of December, the third of January, the third of February); symmetry in space as well . . . Suddenly, he felt as if he were on the point of solving the mystery. A set of calipers and a compass completed his quick intuition. He smiled, pronounced the word Tetragrammaton (of recent acquisition), and phoned the Inspector. He said, "Thank you for the equilateral triangle you sent me last night. It has enabled me to solve the problem. This Friday, the criminals will be in jail, we may rest assured."

"Then they're not planning a fourth murder?"

"Precisely because they are planning a fourth murder, we can rest assured."

Lönnrot hung up. One hour later, he was traveling on one of the Southern Railway's trains, in the direction of the abandoned villa of Triste-le-Roy. To the south of the city of our story flows a blind little river of muddy water, defamed by refuse and garbage. On the far side is a suburb where, under the protection of a political boss from Barcelona, gunmen thrive. Lönnrot smiled at the thought that the most celebrated gunman of all, Red Scharlach, would have given the world to know of his clandestine visit. Azevedo had been an associate of Scharlach; Lönnrot considered the remote possibility that the fourth victim might be Scharlach himself. Then he rejected the idea. He had very nearly deciphered the problem; the mere circumstances, the reality (names, prison records, faces, judicial and penal proceedings), hardly interested him now. He wanted to take a walk, he wanted to rest from three months of sedentary investigation. He reflected on the fact that the explanation of the murders was in an anonymous triangle and a dusty Greek word. The mystery appeared almost crystalline to him now; he was mortified to have dedicated a hundred days to it.

The train stopped at a silent loading station. Lönnrot got off. The air of the muddy, puddled plain was damp and cold.

He saw dogs, he saw a wagon on a dead road, he saw the horizon, he saw a silver-colored horse drinking the crapulous water of a pool. It was growing dark when he saw the rectangular belvedere of the villa of Triste-le-Roy, almost as tall as the black eucalypti which surrounded it. He thought that scarcely one dawning and one nightfall (an ancient splendor in the east and another in the west) separated him from the moment long-desired by the seekers of the Name.

A rust-colored wrought-iron fence defined the irregular perimeter of the villa. The main gate was closed. Lönnrot, without much hope of getting in, circled the area. Once again before the insurmountable gate, he placed his hand between the bars and almost mechanically encountered the bolt. The creaking of the gate surprised him. With a laborious passivity, the whole gate swung back.

Lönnrot advanced among the eucalypti, treading on confused generations of rigid, broken leaves. Viewed from close up, the house of the villa of Triste-le-Roy abounded in pointless symmetries and in maniacal repetitions: to one Diana in a murky niche corresponded a second Diana in another niche, one balcony was reflected in another balcony, double stairways led to double balustrades. A two-faced Hermes projected a monstrous shadow. Lönnrot circled the house, as he had the villa. He examined everything; beneath the level of the terrace he spied a narrow Venetian blind.

He pushed it; a marble stairway descended to a vault. Lönnrot, who had now perceived the delights of the architect, guessed that at the opposite wall there would be another stairway. He found it, ascended, raised his hands, and opened the trap door.

A brilliant light led him to a window. He opened it; a yellow, rounded moon defined two dry fountains in the melancholy garden. Lönnrot explored the house. Through anterooms and galleries he passed to duplicate patios, and time after time to the same patio. He ascended the dusty stairs to circular antechambers; he was multiplied infinitely in opposing mirrors; he grew tired of opening or half-opening windows which revealed outside the same desolate garden from various heights and various angles; inside, only pieces of furniture, wrapped in yellow cases, and chandeliers, bound up in tarlatan. A bedroom detained him; in that bedroom, one single flower in a porcelain vase; at the first touch, the ancient petals fell apart. On the third floor, the top story, the house seemed infinite and expanding. *The house is not this large,* he thought. *Other things are making it seem larger: the dim light, the symmetry, the mirrors, so many years, my unfamiliarity, the loneliness.*

By way of a spiral staircase, he arrived at the oriel. The early evening moon shown through the rhombs of the window; they were yellow, red, and green. An astonishing, dizzying recollection struck him.

Two men of short stature, robust and ferocious, threw themselves on him and disarmed him; another, very tall, saluted him gravely and said, "You are very kind. You have saved us a night and a day."

It was Red Scharlach. The man handcuffed Lönnrot. The latter at length recovered his voice.

"Scharlach, are you looking for the Secret Name?"

Scharlach remained standing, indifferent. He had not participated in the brief struggle, and he scarcely extended his hand to receive Lönnrot's revolver. He spoke; Lönnrot noted in his voice a fatigued triumph, a hatred the size of the universe, a sadness not less than that hatred.

"No," said Scharlach. "I am seeking something more ephemeral and perishable; I am seeking Erik Lönnrot. Three years ago, in a gambling house on the Rue de Toulon, you arrested my brother and had him sent to jail. My men slipped me away from the gun battle in a coupé, with a policeman's bullet in my stomach. Nine days and nine nights I lay dying in this desolate, symmetrical villa; fever gripped me, and the odious two-faced Janus, who watches the twilights and the dawns, lent horror to my dreams and to my waking. I came to abominate my body; I came to sense that two eyes, two hands, two lungs are as monstrous as two faces. An Irishman tried to convert me to the faith of Jesus; he repeated to me the phrase of the *goyim:* All roads lead to Rome. At night, my delirium nurtured itself on that metaphor; I felt that the world was a labyrinth, from which it was impossible to flee, for all roads, though they pretend to lead to the north or south, actually lead to Rome, which was also the quadrilateral jail where my brother was dying and the villa of Triste-le-Roy. On those nights, I swore by the God who sees with two faces and by all the gods of fever and of the mirrors to weave a labyrinth around the man who had imprisoned my brother. I have woven it and it is firm: The ingredients are a dead writer on heresies, a compass, an eighteenth-century sect, a Greek word, a dagger, the rhombs of a paint shop.

"The first object of the sequence was given to me by chance. I had planned with a few colleagues—among them Simon Azevedo—the robbery of the Tetrarch's sapphires. Azevedo betrayed us: He got drunk with the money that we had advanced him and he undertook the job a day early. He got lost in the vastness of the hotel; around two in the morning he stumbled into Yarmolinsky's room. The latter, harassed by insomnia, had started to write. He was working on some notes, apparently, or an article on the Name of God he had already written the words *The first letter of the Name has been uttered.* Azevedo warned him to be silent; Yarmolinsky reached out his hand for the bell, which would awaken the hotel's forces; Azevedo countered with a single stab in the chest. It was almost a reflex action; half a century of violence had taught him that the easiest thing is to kill. Ten days later, I learned through the *Yiddishe Zeitung* that you were seeking in Yarmolinsky's writings the key to his death. I read the *History of the Sect of Hasidim;* I learned that the reverent fear of uttering the Name of God had given rise to the doctrine that that Name is all-powerful and recondite. I discovered that some Hasidim, in search of that secret Name, had gone so far as to commit human sacrifices. . . . I knew that you would make the conjecture that the Hasidim had sacrificed the rabbi; I set myself the task of justifying that conjecture.

"Marcel Yarmolinsky died on the night of December third; for the second sacrifice, I selected the night of January third.

Yarmolinsky died in the north; for the second 'sacrifice' a place in the west was suitable. Simon Azevedo was the inevitable victim. He deserved death; he was impulsive, a traitor; his apprehension could destroy the entire plan. One of us stabbed him; in order to link his corpse to the other one, I wrote on the paint shop diamonds, *The second letter of the Name has been uttered.*

"The third 'murder' was produced on the third of February. It was a mere sham. I am Gryphius-Ginzberg-Ginsburg; I endured an interminable week (supplemented by a trifling fake beard) in the perverse cubicle on the Rue de Toulon, until my friends abducted me. From the running board of the coupé, one of them wrote on the shed, *The last of the letters of the Name has been uttered.* That sentence revealed that the series of murders was *triple.* Thus the public understood it; I, nevertheless, interspersed repeated signs that would allow you, Erik Lönnrot, the reasoner, to understand that the series was quadruple. A portent in the north, others in the east and west, demand a fourth portent in the south; the Tetragrammaton—the name of God, JHVH—is made up of *four* letters; the harlequins and the paint shop sign suggested *four* points. In the manual of Leusden, I underlined a certain passage: the passage manifests that Hebrews compute the day from sunset to sunset; it makes known that the deaths occurred on the *fourth* of each month. I sent the equilateral triangle to Treviranus. I foresaw that you would add the missing point, the point which would form a perfect rhomb, the point which fixes in advance where a punctual death awaits you. I had premeditated everything, Erik Lönnrot, in order to attract you to the solitude of Triste-le-Roy."

Lönnrot avoided Scharlach's eyes. He looked at the trees and the sky, subdivided into rhombs of turbid yellow, green, and red. He felt faintly cold, and he felt, too, an impersonal—almost anonymous—sadness. It was already night; from the dusty garden came the futile cry of a bird. For the last time, Lönnrot considered the problem of symmetrical and periodic death.

"In your labyrinth there are three lines too many," he said at last. "I know of one Greek labyrinth which is a single straight line. Along that line so many philosophers have lost

223

themselves that a mere detective might well do so, too. Scharlach, when in some other incarnation you hunt me, pretend to commit (or do commit) a murder at A, then a second murder at B, eight kilometers from A, then a third murder at C, four kilometers from A and B, halfway between the two. Wait for me afterward at D, two kilometers from A and C, again halfway between both. Kill me at D, as you are now going to kill me at Triste-le-Roy."

"The next time I kill you," replied Scharlach, "I promise you that labyrinth, consisting of a single straight line, which is invisible and unceasing."

He moved back a few steps. Then, very carefully, he fired.